UNDER GROUND

WENDY SMITH

Edited by CREATING INK

Photography by GOLDEN CZERMAK/
FURIOUSFOTOG

Cover Design by GOLDEN CZERMAK/
FURIOUSFOTOG

1

ALEX

The frosty air leaves my lungs aching as I round another corner. Pounding the pavement has become one of my favourite things to do since I came to New Zealand to film this movie. The chilly morning will soon give way to a glorious day full of sunshine, and that's the payoff to my early start.

We're about to begin filming after several weeks of rehearsal, and my routine will change again as I'll be on set by this hour most mornings.

Every day, I've taken a different route around the neighbour-hood. I'm enjoying the variety as I pass different houses, and today's run ends in a park I discovered on the map last night.

At one end of the park is a children's playground, but more importantly, benches to stop and stretch on before I turn back to my rental home.

Brightly coloured playground equipment glistens with dew, but I'm so heated from my run, I barely care as I sit on a wooden bench.

Leaning forward, I stretch out my calf muscles and roll my

shoulders. I'm no fan of running, but it helps clear my head for the day. And I need to be clear on what I'm doing. I've been building up to this movie, and even though it's a smaller role, it's the first one I've had major press for.

Name recognition is hard in this game, but I'm so close to something big, I can smell it.

I stretch my legs out and close my eyes as I raise my face to the sun. It's around seven in the morning, and the sun warms my cheeks. I'm sure that in winter, it gets colder here, but right now I'm enjoying this.

Someone grips my arm. My eyes fly open.

Turning my head, I see a little girl. The sunlight gives her blonde head a halo of light, and her big blue eyes drink me in. Her lips purse, and her light-coloured eyebrows knit as she stares at me.

"Hi." I smile.

Her mouth forms a big O. "Daddy?"

I shake my head. "No, honey. Where did you come from?"

"Casey Maitland. What have I told you ..."

Before I know it, the little girl has crawled around me, and slipped onto my lap, her arms around my neck. I'm not sure how old she is—maybe three? But as I turn to look behind me, where the voice came from, I catch my breath.

This has to be Casey's mother.

With the same big blue eyes and blonde hair, it's her turn to be haloed in the morning light. She's the most beautiful thing I've ever seen.

"Mummy. It's Daddy," Casey says. She says it so matter-of-factly that for a moment, *I* almost believe her. But I've never been to New Zealand before, and there is no way I'd forget this woman.

The woman's cheeks flush bright red, and she shakes her head. Reaching us, she holds out her arms for Casey. "I am so sorry. I've told her a million times not to be so friendly with strangers." Her eyes widen. "Not that I'm saying you're dodgy or anything, it's just ..."

I chuckle and loosen the tight grip around my neck, taking the girl's hands in mine. "I get it." I cock my head. "I'm Alex Stone."

"Yes." The woman presses her lips together in amusement. "I mean. I know who you are. Lana Maitland. And this is Casey."

"Hello, Casey. I'm going to give you back to your mother now."

"Daddy." She wails.

Lana face-palms, then runs her hand down her cheeks. "No, Casey. We have to get going now. It's time to see Maria at day care."

"But, Daddy." Tears—really big drops of tears—stream from this kid's eyes. It's bewildering, but also a little amusing.

"Casey. We need to go."

Wait.

She's not out and out telling the kid I'm not her father. What on earth is this all about?

"Here you go." I stand, swinging Casey onto my hip, and then hand her off to her mother. All Casey does is let out a louder cry and kick her legs.

"I'm so sorry. She's just a little confused. Thank you for not getting too upset."

I shrug. "She's only young. I'd love to know why she's calling me Daddy, though. There's a story, I'm sure."

But I'm not sure I've ever seen anyone so mortified. Her mouth drops open, and her eyes dart from me to Casey and back again. While her cheeks aren't quite as red as they were, they're still a shade of crimson.

"She's just got it really wrong. Sorry to have bothered you."

She turns and walks away, heading toward a large building in the corner of the park. I guess that's where day care is.

I'm glued to the spot, unable to take my eyes off the two blonde angels walking away. Why does that little girl think I'm her father?

She's almost a park length away from me before her cries

become inaudible. She's inconsolable, thrashing in her mother's arms all the way.

What the hell is going on?

I stretch my hamstring and break into a light jog once again.

That was weird, but I don't have time for distractions, beautiful or otherwise.

I have a job to do—and I'm going to nail the hell out of it.

2

———

LANA

If I could force the earth to open up right now and swallow me whole, I'd do it.

I want to die.

Never in a million years did I ever think we'd ever meet Alex Stone in real life. Of all the celebrities in the world, it just had to be him.

"Casey, I told you before. The man in the magazine is not your father," I say as we walk toward the day care.

"No, no, no! Daddy!" she wails and I cringe. Who would have ever thought letting her believe that little white lie—even for a little while—could turn into such a disaster.

But when she picked up the magazine and pointed to the man in the photo and said "Daddy," it had been too hard to correct her.

Her father has never played any part in her life. For some reason, she claimed the man in the article as her father and wouldn't let it go.

At first, I tried to talk to her and tell her that it wasn't her father. But unfortunately, she has all the stubbornness of a three-year-old—one who sees the other kids at day care with their dads and knows hers doesn't live with us.

In the end, I gave up. There wasn't any chance of us ever meeting this random man—the one who was starring in some movie.

Alex Stone.

And yet this morning, there he was in the park we walk through to get to day care.

"Daddy," Casey wails.

I take a deep breath and keep marching toward the big yellow building with the colourful play equipment out the front. I'm filled with regret, but not sure what else I'm supposed to have done.

My cheeks burn with embarrassment as I see the confused look on Alex's face in my mind—over and over again.

It'll be one of those humiliating things I'll think about for years. Maybe when Casey turns twenty-one, we'll look back and laugh. But right now, there's nothing funny about any of this.

Casey thrashes about in my arms, but I know if I let her go, she'll run back to the park and *him*. I don't need that. What just happened is humiliating enough.

Reaching the gate, I drop her to the ground and hold her hand tight. She looks over her shoulder back at the bench seats and screams at me, "Let me go."

"No, Casey. Come on. Let's go and see Maria."

"No Maria. I want Daddy," she screeches. She's so loud, he can probably hear her from here. Hell, her actual dad could probably hear her, what with the noise she's making.

She weeps as we make it first through the gate and then into the building.

Her teacher's standing by the office just inside the door. She takes one look at us, and her brows take off.

"Are we having one of *those* mornings?" Maria is always way too cheerful for this hour of the morning. It takes me at least two coffees to get going once I'm in the office, and even then I'll never be as chirpy as her.

"Daddy." Casey sniffs.

Maria arches an eyebrow at me. She knows my deal—well, some of it. That there's just me, and Casey's father isn't in her life. Maria's been working at the day care since Casey was a baby.

"It's a long story. But Casey just accosted a man in the park, and she's upset about us leaving him behind."

"Ohhh." Maria wrinkles her nose. "Awkward."

"Yeah. It might take a while to distract her this morning. Sorry."

She shrugs and reaches for Casey. "It's fine. We've got some new toys to play with today. I'm sure we'll be okay."

For a moment, I stand there while she leads Casey away. Casey's still sniffing, and I'm the worst mother in the world. Why I didn't stand my ground over her and that damn picture, I'll never know. It was just easier to give up and let her believe what she wanted to.

Maybe if I wasn't alone and I didn't have to do everything by myself, I wouldn't be so damn tired and cave so easily.

"Bye, Casey. Have a good day."

"I've got this," Maria mouths, and tears well in my eyes as I sign the attendance book and walk out the door. The cold air bites, and I close my eyes, soaking in the sun for a moment.

What I want is to turn home and take a day off, but I'm reluctant to use my leave in case I ever really need it.

Instead, I soldier on, making my way around the day care building and out the gate on the other side that faces the road. It makes my walk to work longer, but I can't risk facing Alex again.

I'm not even sure how to explain Casey's tantrum.

She thinks you're her dad because she picked you out of a magazine. Her real dad wants nothing to do with her.

Yeah. Nah.

Alex Stone is gorgeous. He's around six foot of dark hair, and he has blue eyes with scruff that covers his chin. I blush just thinking about him. There's been no man in my life since Casey's dad—that was way too complicated.

It makes for a lonely life, but it's just Casey and me, and she comes first.

And now I'm running late.

Screw it.

Gareth Turner can suck it. It's not like he's got the guts to fire me.

The chilly air slowly warms with the sun shining brightly. I'm no fan of winter, but after the frost in the morning, we do get the most wonderful sunny days.

I walk into the office, past the reception desk in front of the big bay window, and to my not so visible spot in the corner.

"You're late." Of course Gareth is out in the office. It's guaranteed with the luck that I have. He stands with his arms folded, his glare fixed firmly on me.

"Five minutes, and I'm here now. Keep your hair on."

He frowns. It's a sensitive subject given that this past year, he's started balding. The charming, handsome man I thought I was in love with four years ago is long gone, and he knows it. It's not like he's that old—early forties—but maybe all the shitty things he's done over the years are catching up.

"Are you okay? You look flushed," Anna says. She's a sweet girl—fresh out of school and our new receptionist. I watch out for her, even though she doesn't know it. I was her once.

"It's cold out there. And Casey was a bit upset about going to day care this morning."

At the mention of our daughter's name, Gareth scuttles back into his office. It's just as well. I've got a lot of work to do this morning, and I don't need him over my shoulder.

"Aww, poor thing. Is she okay?" Anna's all curly brown hair and dimples, and she has a big heart. I do appreciate her caring.

"She'll be fine. Kids just get funny sometimes."

I round my desk and sit down. For a moment, I have to stop and think hard about what to do next.

Anna chuckles. "Are you okay? You look dazed."

I huff out a breath and nod. "I just need to get myself together. This morning's got me a bit rattled."

"Want a coffee? I was just about to make one."

My shoulders slump, and I smile at her. We've only got each other in this office, and I appreciate the easy friendship that's happened between us.

I started work here in her role four years ago, leaving home at eighteen and getting a job with Gareth as his receptionist right as he struck out on his own as an investment advisor.

It took some time, but last year, he promoted me to office administrator and hired a receptionist. His next step is to lure one of his former co-workers to work with him, but it's a work-in-progress. Or, as he says, he's taking baby steps.

Those baby steps involve a ton of work for me, and I sigh at the thought of my to-do list.

"Wow. You really are a million miles away, aren't you?" Anna picks up the mug from my desk. "I'll take that as a yes."

No. I just wish I was.

By mid-morning, I'm in the thick of it. Gareth's business is doing well, but there are constant reports he wants from me, and from the day I arrived here till now, I've had zero training. It's been my determination and Google that have got me through this.

Thankfully, he's been in his office with a new client for the past hour, and I've been able to get on with it.

He's all smiles as they walk out together, and after his client's gone, he spins on his heel.

"Have you got that sales report?" He glares at me.

"I'm just finishing it up now and it'll be on your desk in the next ten minutes."

He gives me a short, sharp nod and walks back into his office, closing the door.

"He really does have it in for you," Anna says.

I rub my face with my hands. "He's just grumpy. This report was due about half an hour ago."

"Still … it's not the end of the world. The way he looks at you creeps me out."

Clamping my lips together, I look away. It's not worth getting into any of this with someone I don't really know. Maybe it would be easier if I shared the details with her, but my past with Gareth isn't anything I like to talk about if I can avoid it.

"I don't worry about it. He's not great, but I like the work." That's not really quite true either, but as a single mother, I'd rather have job security than end up worse off somewhere else.

"Me too. And I like working with you."

I smile. "I like working with you too." After pinning the last of my documents together, I drop the stapler. "Here goes."

I pick up my collated papers and stand. It'd be so much easier just to email Gareth the documents, but he's a stickler for his paperwork. It's so unnecessary, but he's the boss.

Tapping on his door, I wait a moment.

"Come in," he says.

I open the door and cross the room.

"Here you go." I dump the report on the desk and turn to leave. I get to the door before he speaks.

"Lana. Wait. Close the door."

I suck in a breath, close the door, and turn back.

"I'm sorry if I was a bit short out there. Things are …" He sighs. "Tense with Melanie."

Crossing my arms, I tap my foot. "I'm sorry to hear that, but that's no excuse to take it out on me."

"I agree." He clasps his hands together. "I'd really like a sympathetic ear after work if you're available."

I snort, dropping my hands and shaking my head. "If I'm available? Are you for real?"

He recoils. "I'm just having trouble finding someone who will listen."

"Maybe you should try talking to your wife? I have other priorities."

His gaze drops, and I turn away.

"We can't have children."

I swallow hard. "That's not my problem."

"It's not mine either. But I can't tell Melanie that. The doctors don't know what's wrong. It's frustrating. We're starting IVF."

Sucking in my bottom lip, I close my eyes and give my head a slow, small shake. "I'm sure it is." Clasping my hands together, I take a step forward. "And for what it's worth, I'm sorry for Melanie, if that's what she wants."

"I guess what I'm saying is that we need to be extra careful. If she finds out about …" He pauses, and I know it's because he doesn't want to say Casey's name. It shouldn't hurt, but it does. Despite him not wanting anything to do with her, she's still biologically his daughter.

I drop my hands. "She won't. I might not like you, but your wife is a good person. She deserves better than you."

He clenches his jaw. "I know."

"No one ever needs to know who Casey's father is. We agreed to that, and I have no intention of breaking that agreement."

His lips curl up a little. "I'm glad to hear it."

"I'm not vindictive."

"I know. Which is why I'm drawing up a new contract for you. There's a pay increase included."

My eyebrows rise of their own volition. "You're rewarding me for keeping quiet?"

He stands, makes his way around the desk. In fairness to him, he keeps his distance, but it doesn't stop my skin from crawling.

"I guess so. Melanie's happiness is my priority, and if we're going down the track I think we are, the last thing I need is for her to find out I fathered a child with someone else."

My throat tightens. I'm used to him not wanting anything to do with Casey, but it still hurts when he refers to her in such a distant way. My dad might have chosen his old-fashioned beliefs over me, but he was always my dad.

Casey's never had anyone in that role. No wonder she fought so hard this morning.

Still, it's better that we're alone. Casey and I are so much happier without Gareth in our lives and I have no intention of ever changing that.

"She won't find out from me."

3

LANA

Maybe I'm too sensitive.

But I can't risk another possible run-in with Alex Stone. What if this is his new running route and I see him again?

This morning, I break all my own rules and take the car. It's a rare treat because I live so close to day care and work, so there's usually not much point. Besides, the car just costs money when I use it.

Casey's singing in the back seat, and it makes me smile. She's not said anything more about 'Daddy' but we'll have to have a chat about that over the weekend.

I'm not sure I'll be successful at convincing her Alex isn't her father, but I have to try. Especially when he's in town, and there's a chance we'll run into each other again.

I should have known that was the case from the moment I saw the picture of him in the magazine. The story said he'd be coming here to film, but I didn't think that meant quite literally to the city where we live—right down to the suburb.

"How are we doing this morning?" Maria's smile is so warming. It even makes me feel better, despite the tight knot in my stomach.

"Much better than yesterday. She seems to have forgotten about what happened."

She tilts her head. "Do you really think that's like Casey? She has the best memory of all the kids."

I laugh. "You're right. She'll hit me with it when I least expect it."

Maria takes Casey's hand in hers. "Come on, Casey. I'm helping out in the baby room today. Want to come and say hello?"

Casey grins and nods.

"Have a good day," I say. "Bye, Casey."

For a moment, I just watch as they walk away. This is ridiculous. I have to get back to normal tomorrow and walk. It's not far and pretty crazy to be using the car for this short a distance.

Gareth is out of the office when I get there, which is a welcome relief. He's doing some tax course for a couple of days that I'd forgotten about, but it's nice to have some time when I won't have to worry about his bullshit. And it's nice to get some work done without interruption. The morning flies by, and before I know it, it's after midday. I've got a pile of papers on my desk ready for Gareth when he comes back in tomorrow. If anything, I've managed to get a little ahead.

"Oh. My. God." Anna's voice snaps me out of my thoughts.

"What?"

"Look who's out there."

I look out the front window. There's a man looking in and squinting in my direction.

Shit.

"Alex Stone," she breathes, and I shoot a sideways glance at her.

"What? He's gorgeous."

Shit.

Gareth chose this office because it was central in Havelock North—the most affluent suburb of Hastings. We don't get walk-ins, but he dreams about it happening. And despite the signage on the window, there's still a lot of glass to see through, and we sit out the front.

Alex peers closer, and I know it's too late to hide from the bright smile on his face.

"Oh my god. He's coming in." Anna claps her hands. "Why on earth is he looking at you like *that*?"

"I have no idea," I mutter.

The door opens, and Alex strolls in like he owns the place.

"Lana. It's good to see you."

Why is everything about him so perfect? I guess he's got that Hollywood look. Perfect teeth, perfect hair, perfect dimple in his cheek when he smiles.

I've never felt so plain in all my life in comparison.

"You too." I muster up a smile, but it feels awkward. God only knows what it must look like. Anna bounces up and down, and I can't help but smile. "Anna. This is Alex."

"I know." She squeaks, and I turn my head, one eyebrow raised, to look at her. "I can't wait for your movie to come out."

"Which one?" His puzzled expression just makes him even cuter. Life is *so* unfair.

"The one you're working on now. I love fantasy movies."

"Ohhh." His charming smile is probably enough to knock panties off. Not that I'd know. I'm immune.

At least, that's what I tell myself.

"How's it all going?" she asks.

He nods slowly. "Good. We're just about to start filming, so I'm taking some time to check out the neighbourhood. I've been here a while, but haven't been out much." I swallow hard as he fixes his blue-eyed gaze on me. "Except for my morning runs."

"Great," Anna smiles. "If you need a tour guide ..."

"Oh." He looks back at her. "Thanks for the offer."

"Did you want a coffee? I can make one, or there's a great coffee shop just across the road, or ..."

He pats his stomach—that defined abdomen that I might have seen when I googled him last night. "I've just had a late breakfast and coffee. But thanks for the offer." Shifting his gaze to me, he bites his lip. Holy shit. "I just wanted a word with Lana."

"I ... sure."

Anna doesn't get the hint, God bless her, and stays right where she is.

Alex waits a moment and just focuses on me. "Anyway, I wanted to say I'm glad you're okay."

Oh.

I flick one wrist in the air. "Oh, I'm fine. We were running late today. Really late."

His brows dip. "I didn't want you to think I was upset about yesterday."

"Yesterday?" Anna asks.

I clamp my lips together. *Please don't tell her. Please don't tell her.* The last thing I need are any questions about my daughter.

"Just a little misunderstanding." He flashes another killer smile that makes me suppress a loud sigh. Why did he have to be so good-looking? I'm not used to dealing with men—especially ones like this. It's just too much.

Anna shoots me a wary look that tells me the minute he's gone, I'm going to be interrogated.

"I'm glad. No, we're fine."

"Good." He pauses. "Do you usually walk that way?"

Oh.

"I ... yeah it's the quickest way to get to Casey's day care." I suck in my bottom lip. "I've not seen you there before."

He shrugs. "I've been getting the layout of the neighbourhood. Yesterday was the first time I ran that way."

I nod slowly, unsure of what to say next. Anna nudges my elbow.

"I might see you in the morning?" he asks.

My heart leaps out of my chest and does laps around the office. "Sure."

He smiles. "I guess I'd better let you get back to work."

As he turns, my gaze automatically drops down. His tight jeans are enough to make any red-blooded straight woman sigh. But somehow, I hold that in.

Turning as he opens the door, he makes eye contact again and waves.

It takes everything in me to raise my hand and wave back without losing the plot.

He's just … everything.

As soon as he's gone, Anna spins on her heel and stares at me. "You need to tell me what happened yesterday. The man was practically drooling over you."

I snort. "He was not."

Anna leans against her desk, crossing her arms. "He so was. You lucky, lucky bitch."

Laughing, I sit, rolling my chair closer to my desk and sliding my hand over my mouse to go back to work. "You're imagining things."

"So, what happened?"

I run my free hand through my hair. "I cut through a park to get to day care and he was out for a run yesterday. We ran into each other."

She grins. "How exciting. He's just …" She lets out a sigh that leaves me struggling not to roll my eyes.

But she's right.

He is.

Anna smiles smugly at me before flouncing back to the reception desk and taking her seat.

It takes a lot of effort to hide my smile. Since Casey was born, and without a lot of support, I've hidden away from the world to a certain extent. I've had my routine of *day care, work, day care, home* during the week since she was four months old. And my weekends are spent making up for my lost time with my daughter during the week.

I've not missed dating because I never really dated in the first place. Dad was strict on that, and I leapt into a relationship with the first man to ever really pay me attention once I moved out.

It's left me scars, but it also left me with Casey. She's the reason for my living.

There are times when I miss my parents. We're not on good terms, and being a pregnant, unwed mother was way too much for them to handle. If things were different, I know they'd be supportive and be there for me.

Things aren't different, though. This is my life. And no matter how tough it gets being on my own, I wouldn't swap my life for anything.

I'm sure Alex is just being nice—he's probably still really curious about Casey's reaction to him.

But the thought of him and that killer smile makes me warm inside.

It's a shame nothing will come of us meeting.

The one thing that might happen if we see Alex again, is Casey getting upset all over again.

I need to talk to her again tonight.

4

LANA

I zip up Casey's jacket and tap her on the nose.

"Now, remember what I said last night. We might see Alex in the park. But he is not your father, Casey. He's just a ... man. Okay?"

She purses her lips. "He not my daddy?"

I fight the urge to roll my eyes. We went over this last night, and by the time she went to bed, she seemed to agree with me.

"No, my love. He's not. I think he's a very nice man, but he's not related to you. You can't call him Daddy."

Casey wrinkles her nose. "Okay."

"Good girl." She slides her hand into mine, and I give it a gentle squeeze. "Love you, Casey."

"Love you, Mummy." She giggles and for a moment I can forget everything but the love I have for my daughter. It's everything.

By the time we cross the road and set foot on the edge of the park, there's a giant knot in my stomach.

Please don't be here. Please don't be here. Please don't ...

"Daddy!" Casey yells.

I blow out a long, slow breath. She tugs her hand out of mine and runs, launching herself at Alex so he has no option *but* to catch her.

Coming to a halt, I facepalm.

Oh, Casey. No.

I run after her. "I am *so* sorry."

His lips curl into a smile. "Don't be. I was hoping to run into you two."

"Really? I thought you'd be running in the opposite direction."

Alex laughs. "After yesterday? I had to see you again. Both of you." He shoots me a pointed look as if to reassure me he really does mean both of us.

He tries to lower Casey to the ground, but she's not budging.

"Maybe today before you run off, you can tell me why Casey here calls me Daddy."

Casey giggles.

"She saw you in a magazine and decided ..." I chew on my bottom lip rather than finish that particular sentence. Just the thought makes my cheeks flush.

"That I was ..."

I nod.

Despite neither of us saying it, the way he tilts his head and briefly closes his eyes tells me he gets it.

"Well, I was wondering if you'd like to go out to dinner sometime. Maybe you can tell me the full story about this one." He nods toward Casey, and she takes the opportunity to grab hold of his face and kiss his cheek.

My heart thuds. "I'm not really one for going out ..."

His mouth falls open. "I'm sorry. I didn't see a wedding ring."

My eyes widen. "Oh, no. I'm not married. It's just that it's only me and Casey. I don't get out."

He nods slowly. "My mom was the same. She always says she never had a social life until I was old enough to leave home alone."

Despite myself, I laugh. "That sounds about right."

Casey buries her face in Alex's neck. This should be awkward, but there's something magical about it. It's not like I had any choice about her father's lack of involvement in her life, and to see her like this is heart-warming.

Even if it's a little weird.

But maybe he can help me convince her that he's not really her father.

Besides, he seems like a good guy and he seems interested.

It can't hurt to spend more time with him—If that's what he wants.

I lick my lips. "Why don't you come around for dinner one night?"

"I'd like that."

I can't help but smile. "Great. Are you free Saturday?"

"I'm free every evening at the moment. We're starting filming this week, and night shoots are some time away."

I face-palm as Casey slaps a big sloppy kiss on his cheek, but Alex just laughs.

"Casey." I groan. "Let's make it Saturday, maybe around six, and we can talk about this situation."

He turns his head to look at her. "Thank you, Casey. I should let you go now."

This time, he manages to lower her to the ground and she beams up at him.

"How about you give me your number and I'll text you for the address?" he asks.

My cheeks burn. It's not the first time I've been asked for my number, but it is the first time I've wanted to give it out. "Sounds good."

His dimple pops when he smiles. It's so cute, I could ...

"What's your number?"

"Uhh." I give it to him, and he taps it into his Apple watch.

My phone buzzes in my bag, and I fish it out. Alex grins. "Just reply to that and I will be there on Saturday at six as arranged."

"Great." My heart pounds. "We should go or I'll be late. Casey, we'll see Alex on Saturday."

Please let this be enough to stop her from getting upset.

"Bye, Daddy." She waves, her whole face alight with glee. I'm not sure I've ever seen her so happy.

I scratch behind my ear, still uncomfortable with this whole thing, but Alex doesn't seem to mind.

"Bye, Casey. Have a good day at day care." He shifts his gaze to me. "I'm not sure if I'll be here in the morning, but if not, I'll see you on Saturday."

"Okay."

As he jogs off with one last wave, I give a little sigh just watching him. He's one gorgeous man, *and* he seems to be interested.

"Mummy, come on." Casey slides her hand into mine and tugs at it.

Looking down at her, all I see is a little girl content in her world. I'm still not sure whether contact with Alex is just encouraging her fantasy, but she's happy, and that's all I've ever wanted.

Even if it's fleeting, it's not going to hurt her to have Alex around. But we really do need to knock this whole 'calling him Daddy' thing on the head. The last thing we need is for anyone to pick that up given Alex is a public figure.

Because no matter what, that's in the back of my mind the whole time.

He might not be a superstar yet, but after Anna's reaction, I know that Alex is recognisable in public.

How will I handle it if Casey calls him Daddy in front of other people—in front of the media?

5

ALEX

What am I doing?

Regardless of what we tell her, Casey's got it in her head that I'm her father. I'm not sure you can talk logic into a three-year-old.

And I get it. When I was her age, I was curious about my dad, I'm sure. I still don't know who he was—Mom would never talk about it. Casey just took it to her next level and claimed a random person as her dad.

Even without that on my mind, the chances of me staying away from Lana Maitland are nil. I see her flushed cheeks, her reaction to me, and it's not all to do with Casey.

If I'm not mistaken, she's as attracted to me as I am to her.

I didn't come here looking for love—not even for a fling, but tonight could change all that.

I take a deep breath and knock on the door.

It only takes a moment for it to click, and Lana's there. Her blonde hair hangs down to just past her shoulders, and she's wearing jeans with a figure-hugging light blue shirt on top.

"Hey." She smiles. "Come in."

Hers and Casey's shoes are beside the door, so I kick mine off and step inside. "Hi."

Her cheeks are pink, but I'm not sure if it's because of me or the fact that it's warm in here. The air is filled with the mouth-watering scent of some kind of meat dish.

"Thank you for coming. Casey's been talking about it all day." She tilts her head. "I thought maybe we could have dinner and then talk with her?"

I shrug off my jacket. "Sounds good. Where is she?"

"In her room playing. I'll tell her you're here in a minute." She digs her hands into her jeans pockets. "To tell you the truth, I'm kinda surprised you're here. Most men would run at a little girl throwing themselves at them and calling them Daddy."

I grin. "I'll admit I thought it was odd. But the more I learn about you two, the more I get it. I was Casey once—I never knew my dad."

She drops her gaze. "I'm sorry to hear that."

"Don't be. It was hard at times when I was a kid, and I still wish I knew something about him. But that's not likely to happen anytime soon. I get how Casey feels, but I don't want to mislead her any more than you do. So, if I can help Casey …"

Her lips twitch. "Thank you."

"Daddy!"

I spin in the direction of the screech from behind me. A little blonde hurricane comes flying at me, and I catch her as she jumps.

"Oh my God. Casey. Alex, I am so, so sorry."

The resignation's clear in Lana's tone. She's tried to stop this, but I think little Casey is an unstoppable force, and I understand better than she realises.

"It's okay. Hi, Casey."

Casey buries her face in my neck and I turn around to look at

Lana. Her hand is raised to her face, covering her eyes as if she's exasperated.

"We've gone from 'don't talk to strangers' to 'adopt one off the street'." She lowers her arm, a lopsided smile on her lips.

"Just as well it was me. Not all strangers are nice guys."

She swallows hard and nods. "I know. I'm grateful for that."

Reaching for Casey, she pries her out of my arms and lowers her to the floor. "Honey, leave Alex alone. He just got here."

"But I miss Daddy."

"Well, I'm here now, and we're going to have some dinner. We need to have a chat, Miss Casey," I say.

Lana wrings her hands together. She's nervous, but I'm going to do my best to put her at ease. I'm no psychologist, but I don't think there's anything wrong with Casey. She needs some understanding, and I have plenty.

Casey sits on the couch, and Lana smiles. "Dinner's probably ready. I'll just go and check on it."

I trail behind her, entering a small kitchen. My apartment back home is tiny, but hers isn't much bigger for the two of them. I clamp my lips shut because Lana doesn't need my judgment.

"I didn't ask you if you were a vegetarian or anything." Lana raises her palms to cover her face. "You can tell I'm not used to having people over."

I reach for her arm and pull one of her hands away. She blinks rapidly, and tingles spread up my arm. "I'll eat anything. Don't you worry about me."

"Are you sure?"

"I know I'm gonna need a bite of whatever that is you're cooking in the oven because it's making me drool."

Her wide smile brightens the room. "I'm glad I didn't get that wrong, then."

"You know, even if I was a vegetarian, I'd probably still eat anything you cooked to impress you."

Lana laughs. "That's very sweet, but completely unnecessary."

"Thank you for inviting me over." I bow my head slightly to get a closer look at her.

"Thank you for not upsetting Casey. I know she needs to understand the truth, and I did try to make her see reason, but ..."

"You can't reason with a three-year-old." I finish her sentence, and she screws up her face.

"No, you can't. I just never thought we'd ever run into you. I thought maybe she'd get old enough to talk her out of it and then we'd be fine."

I stroke my chin. "I guess I really screwed up your plans then."

"Yes, but I'm not complaining." Her cheeks pink up. "Dinner's nearly ready if you want to go back to the living room. We don't do anything formal here."

"Whew." I wipe my forehead with the back of my hand.

"It's difficult to when you don't have a dining room. Or a dining table, for that matter." Lana waves me away. "Go, sit, and I'll get us some food."

Casey's watching television when I walk back in, and she looks up and grins as I sit beside her on the couch.

"What are you watching?" I ask.

"It's *Paw Patrol*, Daddy."

"Is that right?"

For the first time since I met her, her focus isn't on me—it's completely on the television. But I get to observe the happy little girl who's so very intriguing.

I always thought about having kids in an abstract sense. It would probably happen eventually. But my focus these past few years has been on my career, although I wasn't actively trying not to settle down.

Now I have these two come into my life in the most unexpected way, and it's got me thinking.

"Here we go. I won't be offended if you don't clear the plate."

Lana laughs. She hands me a plate piled high with meat and gravy, roasted potatoes, peas and beans.

"This looks amazing. Thank you."

"I'll just grab mine and Casey's, and we'll get eating."

"I gotta sit in my chair," Casey says to me.

"Which one is your chair?"

She leaps up and runs to the corner of the room, dragging a Disney Princess chair to the coffee table. "This one."

Lana walks back in with two plates in hand, placing the smaller one on the table in front of Casey before joining me on the couch.

"Dig in." Her smile lights up the room. I've never been so glad to have been in the right place at the right time as I was when I met her.

I moan as that first bite hits me. Tender lamb with gravy never tasted so good. I'm usually pretty good when it comes to eating—I keep in shape for being on-screen, but I clean my plate and could do another one.

"That was amazing," I say.

Lana smiles. "I'm glad you liked it. I wanted to do something special given everything we've put you through."

I grin. "You haven't put me through anything. It's made for an interesting week."

"And an embarrassing week."

I shake my head. "No. You shouldn't be. You just have a three-year-old with an imagination."

She leans closer and lowers her voice. "Thank you for dealing with it the way you have. She'd have been devastated if you'd rejected her."

"I could never have done that."

I find myself staring into her eyes. She says nothing, but her gaze locks me in, and I can't look away. There's a connection between us that I can't explain. It's more than Casey bringing us together, and I can't help feeling this is meant to be.

What I do know is that I want to get to know Lana better.

Swallowing hard, I stand. "I'll help with the dishes."

Lana shakes her head, rising from the couch. "It'll take a couple of minutes to load the dishwasher."

She reaches for my plate and our hands brush. Her eyes meet mine again, and I'm lost in a sea of blue. Lana Maitland is a beautiful woman, but this close? She's spectacular.

My heart thuds.

"Uhh. I'll be back shortly." She turns away, and picks up Casey's empty plate. Her cheeks are flushed, and she takes one last look at me from under her eyelashes and carries the plates into the kitchen.

"Go and wash your hands, Casey," she calls.

"My hands are clean." Casey holds them up for me to inspect. There are smudges of food on them, and I can't help but smile.

"They look like they need a wash to me."

She wrinkles her nose. "No. They clean."

"I don't think so. Good try." I wink at her, and she giggles. "You should go do what your mom wants."

Casey licks the palm of each hand. "All done."

"Casey, are you licking your hands again?" Lana calls. "If you go wash your hands, I'll get you an ice cream for dessert."

Her eyes widen. She uses the table to push herself to her feet and sets off running up the hallway.

I laugh. "That worked."

"It always does."

Before Casey returns, Lana walks back into the living room, an ice cream in a cone in her hand. It's only a small amount of the dessert, but clearly Casey's eager to get her hands on it. "Do you want one too?" Lana asks.

I laugh. "I'm good, thanks."

"Mummy, you give Daddy my ice cream?"

Lana laughs as Casey runs back in. "No, honey. This one is all yours." She hands it to her.

Casey eats while Lana sits next to me. We sit in silence as Casey devours her ice cream and beams at the both of us.

"Be back," Casey yells, launching herself up the hallway.

I laugh. "She's so full of energy."

"She never stops." Lana leans back in her seat.

Casey comes running in with something in her hand. "I got it."

"What do you have there?" I ask.

"My Daddy photo," Casey says.

"Show me."

She raises it to my eye level, and I pluck her from the floor, seating her between Lana and me on the couch.

It's weird—she's got this photo of me, obviously torn from a magazine and framed.

I take it from her outstretched hand and run my thumb over the glass. "This is one well-loved picture."

Casey beams.

"I suggested the frame because she would have been devastated if it had been destroyed." Lana hovers. I'm sure she's worried I'll say the wrong thing—whatever that is, and upset Casey. But that's the last thing I want.

I smile at her. "Good choice. How about you take a photo of me and Casey to replace it?"

She blinks rapidly. "You ... you'd do that?"

"Obviously one day she'll understand, but she'll always have a photo of the time we met."

Tears appear in her eyes, and I can't look away. Lana Maitland is such a beautiful woman, and the thought of making her cry rips me apart. Even if it's because I'm doing a good thing.

"This is just so sweet," Lana says.

I lower my voice. "Casey's not at fault. She knows what she doesn't have and she wants it. Can't blame her for that."

She shifts her gaze to Casey. "Honey, would you like to take a photo with Alex?"

Casey nods, her blue eyes wide.

Lana holds up her phone, and Casey snuggles into my side. I slip an arm around her and smile until Lana nods.

"All done."

Casey reaches for Lana's phone, and Lana brings it over to show her.

She beams. "It's Daddy and Casey."

"I'll get this printed and we can put it in your frame. Okay?" Lana's smile is so loving.

Casey nods, hugs my arm and leaps off the couch. "I'm going to get my toys."

I gaze at the door she runs through for a moment. She's so happy, and it makes my heart swell. "She's a good kid."

Lana sits on the couch beside me and stretches out her legs. "She is."

I turn my head and meet her gaze. Her blonde hair is as fine and wispy as Casey's is, and I want so badly to reach out and brush a stray lock off her face. Instead, I draw in a breath. "You're doing an amazing job all on your own. I know it must be hard."

Lana shrugs. "It's not easy, but we have our routine, and if we keep to that, we're okay." She looks at me from under her long lashes. "Thank you for everything."

I drink her in. She has such pixie-like features, I'm not really sure if she's real. "You're welcome."

Casey's back in an instant, introducing me to a handful of toys in such a whirl, I'll never remember any of their names.

"Casey, we need to talk to you about Alex," Lana says.

Casey stares at her mother. "Daddy?"

Lana draws in a deep breath. "Casey, Alex isn't your dad. You need to stop calling him that."

I place my hand on Lana's arm. "I'd love a little girl like you, but your mom's right."

Casey crosses her arms. "Daddy."

"No, honey." Lana reaches for her and pulls her into her arms. Her shoulders slump, and she lets out a big sigh.

"You not Daddy?" She looks at me.

I shake my head. "I'm not your daddy, sweet girl."

"No. Not *my* daddy. But you're Daddy."

Lana and I exchange glances. I'm not sure we'll make sense of this, but she seems to know what she's talking about.

"You know Alex isn't your father?" Lana asks.

Casey nods, pursing her lips and wrinkling her nose.

Lana lets her go, and she walks to my side and climbs up on the couch beside me, hugging my arm. "Daddy."

I chuckle. "Uhh, she knows exactly what she's doing, you know."

"I know." Lana raises her hand to cover her mouth.

"I'm not sure what to do now." I clamp my lips together.

Lana snorts. "Me either."

She stands and holds out her hand. "It's time to brush teeth and get pyjamas on now anyway. Come on, Casey."

She drags herself away from my side and slides her hand into Lana's.

"How about when you come back, I'll read you a story?" I ask.

Casey jumps up and down. "Yes, please, Daddy."

Lana glances at me over her shoulder as they leave the room, an amused smile on her lips. I'm not sure anything's really changed, but at least we've managed to establish that Casey doesn't actually think I'm her father.

I think.

Casey's excitement means it takes a while for her to wind down, but Lana leaps on her the moment she starts yawning.

"It's time for bed, Casey. Say goodnight to Alex."

She pouts. "But I want to play."

"I know you do. But I'm sure we'll see each other again really soon and we can play then. Okay?" I say.

Lana stares at me, and for a moment I'm not sure if I've overstepped my mark. She seems to force a smile before scooping Casey off the floor and onto her hip. "That sounds wonderful."

There's a wistfulness to her tone, and it hits me. She's not angry at me for overstepping, but I'd bet anything she's thinking about Casey's absent father.

"Let's say goodnight." Lana dips Casey in front of me, and that sweet little girl reaches out and grabs my shirt.

"Goodnight, sweetheart," I say.

Casey's grip tightens. "Goodnight, Daddy."

She kisses me on the cheek before Lana leads her out of the room and up the hallway.

While she's gone, I take the time to look around the room. Casey's everywhere from the photos on every shelf to the small collection of toys in the corner. The two of them are very close, and it makes me a little homesick—more for my mom than any actual home. With my job and her travelling around, I don't see her often.

I'm not even sure if she knows I'm in New Zealand.

I should call her.

Lost in thought, I know Lana's returned to the room when a soft floral scent hits me. She stands in front of the couch, clasping her hands together awkwardly.

"Want a coffee? I only have instant."

I hold up my hands. "Instant is fine with me."

Lana bites her bottom lip. "Really? I thought you'd want something fancy given you're the big movie star."

Wait. She's flirting with me. "I'm far from that."

"Could have fooled me, the way Anna freaked out about you."

She walks past me and into the kitchen, and I turn to watch her. Her shyness seems to have evaporated with Casey no longer around. I guess the whole situation made her nervous—not that it's really been resolved.

"How do you take it?" she calls.

"Black, one sugar."

It only takes a minute more and then she's walking back into the living room, handing me a cup. "Here you go."

Lana sits on the other end of the couch.

I take a sip of coffee and sigh. "Damn, that hits the spot. Now, tell me about you. I want to know your story."

She runs a hand through her hair and sighs. "There's not that much to tell."

"Tell me anyway?"

Closing her eyes briefly, she smiles. "I grew up on a farm not that far from here. My parents were really strict. I had no real idea about the real world, but I left school and got out of home so fast. I was lucky, and I got a job with Gareth. He owns the business you visited the other day." Lana grips her coffee cup. "I was eighteen when I went to work for him. I'd never had a boyfriend before ..."

I fist one hand before I realise I've done it. It's not hard to see what's coming.

"Gareth was much older, but he was so charming, and I got swept up in his attention. I was already pregnant by the time I found out he was married." She closes her eyes and draws in a deep breath. "He wanted me to terminate, but I said no. So, he signed away any parental rights he had to Casey."

She places her coffee mug onto the table and seems to force a smile. I reach for her hand. "What an asshole."

"I'm estranged from my family because they couldn't deal with me being an unmarried mother, so ..." She takes another deep breath. "I'm still working for him because my job's secure. He can't afford for people to find out about Casey, and I'm happy with that."

"That's a shitty situation."

Lana shrugs, her eyes fixed on mine. "I know that, but I have Casey and she's worth it. I'll take that over him being a bigger part of my life."

"You're amazing."

She drops her gaze. "I'm just doing what I have to."

"So, this whole Casey thing ..."

Lana laughs softly. "She's never had her father in her life. And no father figure, thanks to my dad not wanting to know us. But when she saw you in that magazine..." She raises her gaze to the ceiling and sighs. "I'm not sure why you, but it was instant. Maybe it was because you both have blue eyes, because I can't see any other physical resemblance. I don't know." She meets my gaze again. "And I tried to talk her out of it and explain you weren't her father, but she wouldn't have a bar of it. You were it."

My eyebrows arch. "She's very attached."

Lana nods. "She is. It was uncomfortable when it was just us who knew about it, and then somehow we end up running into you."

"Must have been fate."

She snorts. "I'm not sure I believe in that."

"Looks like Casey does."

"Casey believes in Santa and the Easter Bunny too." Lana leans back. "Thank you for everything. It would have been so easy for you to push her away, but you didn't. This whole thing is awkward, but I know it could have been worse for her."

I look down at our still joined hands, and as if she notices them for the first time, Lana pulls her hand away.

"You're welcome. I wouldn't want to break her heart." Our gazes are locked, and I couldn't shift mine even if I wanted to.

Her lips twitch. "You're a good man."

"Just as well, seeing as Casey seems to have adopted me."

Lana breaks eye contact, looking down at her lap. "She definitely knows her own mind. That's for sure."

"I'm glad she found me. I wouldn't have met you otherwise."

She runs her palm along her forehead and down her cheek as if she's flustered. And maybe she is, but it's the most enchanting thing ever. "Alex, I—"

"I'm not unhappy that we met. Are you?"

A grin lights her face. "No."

"She did us a favour." I take a sip of coffee and shrug.

We sit in silence for a while, just drinking our coffee. It's not uncomfortable. But it gives me time to spend with Lana. She buries her nose in her drink, glancing up at me every so often. It's endearing.

I place my cup on the table. "I should get going. I've got an early start tomorrow. Thank you for a lovely evening."

"You're welcome."

"I'm sorry we didn't completely solve your issue with Casey."

Lana sighs. "She's one stubborn kid."

I stand, and she follows suit, then walks to the door with me. As I open it, the chilly night air makes her shiver. "There's just one more thing I want to ask you before I go."

Her lips curl into a smile. "What is it?"

"When can I see you again?"

Her eyes grow wide—I've caught her off-guard. But this is so much more than Casey's attachment to me now. I like Lana. She's gorgeous, smart, and she's tough. I admire that more than anything.

"You want to see me again?"

"I do."

She glances back toward the hallway. "You know any date with me includes my three-year-old."

I run my hands through my hair. "So, no chance of getting a babysitter for next Saturday night? I want to take you to dinner."

She clasps her hands together, her brow furrowing. "I can try."

You're not getting out of it that easy. "If not, we can work something out, I'm sure. That's if you want to see me."

Her lips twitch. "Yes. I think I'd like that very much."

I reach up and push that stray strand of her hair back behind her ear. Her eyes flash with surprise before a shy smile emerges.

"Text me when you're ready. Either way," I say.

She nods, and I take a step back.

"Make sure you lock the door. Take care. Both of you." I pause for a moment to take one last look at her just in case she doesn't call. This whole thing must be weird for her. She clearly didn't think I'd be okay with the way Casey reacted to me.

But Casey's looking for a fatherly connection—one I never had.

I understand that better than anyone.

6

LANA

The thought of dating hasn't crossed my mind since before Casey was born. The last thing I wanted was another man in my life to complicate things, and the last thing I needed was to be left high and dry. Again.

And then there was Casey. At first, she was this little baby who cried all the time, and between exhaustion and leaky boobs, there was no way I was interested in even thinking about men.

As she's grown, she's remained the centre of my world. I'm the one person responsible for this tiny human, and I'm all she has.

Maria once told me that if I ever needed a babysitter, she'd be happy to do it. And it's tough to think about it this way, but she's the only person I can probably ask.

Besides, Casey loves Maria. She's spent almost as much time with her as she has with me in her short life so far, which makes me sad, but also makes me appreciate that we have her.

Both of them light up when they see each other in the morning. It seems the perfect answer.

"Maria!" Casey yells as we walk in the door on Monday.

That. That's what gives me the confidence to ask what I'm

about to, even though nerves are eating my stomach alive. Not because I'm worried about what she'll say, but more because if she accepts, then I'm going on this date.

"Hi there, Miss Casey," Maria says. "Are you ready for lots of fun?"

"Yes." Casey jumps up and down.

"Have a good day." Maria smiles at me.

I suck on my bottom lip. "Actually, I wondered if I could ask you a favour? I wondered if you would babysit for me on Saturday night."

Maria beams. "I'd love to. Does this mean you have a date?" She nudges my arm.

"I do." My cheeks heat up, but I can't help it.

"Good for you. What time?"

Oh. "I'm not sure yet. I have to say yes first."

Her expression softens. "Say yes. I'm always happy to take care of Casey."

"Thank you so much. I should get to work."

There's a spring in my step as I make the ten-minute walk from day care to work.

Maybe things are looking up.

I HAVE REPORTS TO COLLATE, but instead, I browse websites looking for a dress for Saturday. Gareth's out of the office for the day, and I'll deal with his bullshit tomorrow.

I'm not sure what I'm doing.

I don't want anything too fussy—though I also don't know what I want, which is half the problem.

"That was a big sigh," Anna says.

I lean back in my seat. "I've got a date on Saturday night and nothing to wear. I'm not sure what to do."

"Where are you going?"

I shrug. "I don't know. Apparently, the dress code is smart casual. I don't even know what that means."

She rolls her eyes and shakes her head. "You, Lana Maitland, are a lost cause. I'll help you. We're about the same size. I'll nip home at lunchtime and bring you back some things to try on."

I shake my head. "Oh, no, you don't have to do that."

Anna crosses her arms. "That's what friends are for. Besides, I want to see you all dressed up. Who's the lucky guy?"

My cheeks burn. "I ..."

Her eyes widen. "Alex Stone?"

I raise my gaze to avoid meeting her eyes. "Yes?"

She squeals. "Then we are putting in *all* of the effort. Lucky bitch."

"Thank you."

She shrugs. "If I'm not going to get a look in with him, I might as well help you. Besides, I bet he has some cute friends. Maybe famous ones."

I frown. "I know he's famous, but exactly how famous is he?"

Her eyebrows arch. "You really have to ask that? I guess you're not dating him because of who he is."

"I knew who he was, but I don't even know if I've seen him in anything."

She rolls her eyes and sighs. "Totally wasted on you." Laughing, she sits at her desk. "But seriously, he's really on the way up. Especially now there are rumours he'll be cast in Josh Carter's new movie."

Josh Carter. Now there's a name I recognise. He was in a movie on TV a while ago that I did watch because I saw it had won a ton of awards. I sobbed my eyes out at it. "Really?"

"You don't know much about your new boyfriend, do you?"

I shrug. "He's not my boyfriend."

"Yet."

By the time we get to midday and Anna goes home to get some clothing, I'm itching to talk to Alex. An empty office provides the perfect opportunity.

I only hope he answers. Because my conversation with Anna has plagued my thoughts since this morning.

Me: *Can I ask you something before we go on this date?*

It only takes a moment for my phone to start ringing, and I smile at his name. It gives me butterflies even though we're not really anything to each other. Maybe friends at a stretch.

"Alex."

"Please don't tell me you're cancelling."

I smile to myself. "No. I'm just trying to get in time."

"What can I do to help?"

I laugh. "Nothing. But I do want to ask you something."

"Sure."

"Are you likely to get recognised?"

Alex pauses, and my heart drops. The last thing I want is for any attention to end up on Casey and me. We're in a delicate enough situation as it is without anyone going digging. But Alex is just so easy to be around, and I don't really want to call this off before it gets started.

"I don't think so. The only person who's recognised me since I got here is that woman you work with. I think we'll be okay."

That gives me more reassurance than he probably realises, but I'm still a little nervous about the whole thing. "You know why I'm asking, don't you? I don't want Casey exposed to anyone —there are real consequences if people go digging into her background."

He's quiet for a moment. "I know. You want to protect your ex."

"Not him. His wife." I chew my bottom lip. "It's not the easiest situation. I couldn't bring myself to tell her about Casey at first, and then things dragged on so long I didn't even know where to start, and she's dealing with some other things right now, and it'd kill her if she found out he has a child with someone else. Besides, she likes me."

"You're a good person, Lana. I hope you know that."

"I try." The front door clicks, and Anna walks in, one arm laden with clothing. "Anyway, I need to get going. Talk to you later?"

"Anytime. If I'm filming, just leave a message and I'll call you back."

"Will do."

"See you on Saturday. Around six?"

I can't wipe the grin from my face. "See you then."

Disconnecting the call, I place my phone on my desk and look up at Anna's excited expression. She waves the armful of clothing in the air. "I got some things that I think will really suit you. Not too over the top, because I didn't think you'd want to go too over the top. But subtle and sexy."

I cradle my head in my hands. "I'm so glad I have you, because I have no idea."

She chuckles. "I figured. I've never known you to go out with anyone."

"I'm not one to date. It's tough when you have a three-year-old. I barely get much time to myself, let alone spending time with someone else."

Placing the clothes on my desk, she holds up her palms. "Well, then I'll just have to be your fairy godmother." She picks up a silver sparkly top. "Let's start with this one."

ABOUT HALFWAY THROUGH the pile of clothes, I try on a dress.

It's made from a black stretchy fabric and has long sleeves— perfect for the winter weather—and it has a scooped neck which doesn't reveal too much. It comes down to about halfway down my thighs. A pair of black stockings on underneath should complete the look *and* keep me warm. The bathroom mirror isn't the best, but I like this.

And Anna's mouth falls open when I walk back into the office.

"That. Is. It," she says. "You look amazing."

"Really? I thought it was practical."

"You'll knock him dead in that."

The front door opens, and Anna and I exchange a wide-eyed glance as Gareth and Melanie walk in.

Gareth comes to a halt, his eyebrows rising as he looks at me.

"We didn't think you'd be back today," Anna says.

"So I gather." He looks around the office. Anna gathers the clothing on my desk up and starts shoving it in bags.

"Oh, leave them alone, Gareth." Melanie breezes past him. "Lana, you look lovely. Is that a new dress?"

"Just something I'm borrowing from Anna."

Anna beams. "Lana has a date with Alex Stone."

Melanie's eyes crinkle at the corners, and I'm pretty sure she has no idea who Anna's talking about. Which is a relief, in more ways than one.

"He's an actor. Anna's a fan," I say.

Melanie claps her hands. "Sounds exciting. Well, that dress looks so good on you."

I smooth the dress down my thighs. "Thank you."

"Doesn't she look amazing, Gareth?" Melanie clings to his arm, and my shoulders tense. This stopped being so awkward a long time ago when we made our agreement to only have a professional relationship.

"You look fantastic, Lana." Gareth's gaze runs down the length of my body, and my skin prickles in discomfort.

"I appreciate all the kind words. I'll just go and get changed, and we'll get back to work."

"That's it, Lana. That's the dress," Anna calls as I make my way into the bathroom, my cheeks burning.

As if I needed that to happen.

It's a relief when it's time to go home, and even more of one when Casey and I finally walk in the door to our small brick flat.

I reach into my bag and pull the dress out of it before dumping it on the couch. Shaking it, I smile.

"You got some new clothes, Mummy?" Casey stares with wide eyes. I live in jeans when I'm not wearing a skirt and shirt for work. This goes to show just how novel me wearing a dress will be.

"I did. I'm going out on Saturday with Alex, and Maria is going to come here to stay with you."

Her eyes widen even farther. This is unheard of, and for a moment, I bite my bottom lip, awaiting her reaction.

A smile breaks out on her lips, and she claps, spinning around. "Yay! Maria."

Whew.

"You go out with Daddy? Can I come?"

I laugh. "Not this time, sweetheart. But we'll see him another time together."

She purses her lips, and for a moment, it looks like she's going to lose it. Instead, she spins on her heel. "I gots to play with my toys now."

"You do that. I'll start dinner."

For a moment, I watch as she tears off up the hallway. God, how I love this kid with all my heart. That conversation could have easily gone in a whole different direction, but I'm glad it didn't.

Nerves still keep my stomach occupied, but I'm excited. I've never really been on a date, and this certainly qualifies.

Things escalated in the office with Gareth, and it wasn't until I found out later about him being married that it suddenly made sense as to why we didn't go out anywhere together.

Instead, he spent a lot of time at my flat.

The flat that is now home to me and my daughter.

I wish I had the money to move and give her a better home. We play in the park because there are four flats on this property and very little in the way of lawn or garden.

But I also make sure she never wants for anything.

It feels weird doing something for me, and that's what this date feels like.

Maybe it's something that's way overdue.

7

ALEX

Nerves eat at my stomach.

I love living in Los Angeles. Apart from it being *the* place for my career, I've always had an active social life there. But nothing has prepared me for tonight.

Lana opens the door, and I catch my breath.

Her blonde hair is swept up onto her head, and those crystal-blue eyes meet mine with a warmth that sends shivers down my spine.

I'm not imagining things. This attraction is mutual, and it's strong.

"Hi. Come in out of the cold. I'm running a little late, but I'll just finish getting ready."

"Take your time. I'm early, I think." I step in, and she closes the door behind me.

"Daddy." Casey comes running at me, and before I have a chance to respond, she clings to my leg.

"I'll just be a few minutes." Lana touches my arm, and I catch my breath at her shy smile.

"You must be Alex." An older woman rises from the couch. "I'm Maria."

"Maria is sitting on me tonight," Casey says.

Maria laughs. "I'm babysitting, Casey. Not sitting on you."

Casey lets go and thrusts her index finger into her mouth, still looking up at me.

"I'm taking your mom out somewhere real nice for dinner, and then I'll bring her straight back to you," I say, ruffling Casey's hair.

She drops her hand, giggles, and buries her face in my leg. I love that she's so comfortable with me—that has to be a good thing in Lana's book, but it's her mother I'm out to impress.

"Right. I'm ready." Lana appears in the doorway leading to the hall, and I let go of a long breath. She's wearing a long-sleeved black dress that ends about halfway down her thighs. It hugs her figure as if it were made especially for her—maybe it was.

She's wearing light makeup, enough to highlight the blue of her eyes, and her hair is swept up onto her head in a tight bun.

I already find her beautiful, but right now, she's breathtaking.

"I ... uhhh ..."

Maria laughs. It's soft, but I hear it, and I raise one eyebrow as I turn my head to look at her, and she grins at me in return.

"Let's get going," I say, returning my gaze to Lana.

There's only one thing I know at this moment in time.

I'm an insanely lucky man.

"WHERE ARE WE GOING?" she asks, as we make our way through Havelock North and toward Te Mata Peak.

It might be a small town, but it punches above its weight as far as restaurants and wineries are concerned. Once I found out about the place we're going to, I couldn't think of anywhere better. "Peak House."

She smiles. "I've always wanted to go there. I've just never been sure about taking Casey fancy places."

"I'm sure she'd love it. But I'm glad it's just us." I change gear and shoot another glance at her.

"Me too." She sucks in an audible breath and places her hand on top of mine. It's a bold move coming from her, but I love it. Her hand lingers there for a moment before she removes it, but it gives me the signal that tonight's special for her. It makes me all the more determined to make it better than her wildest dreams.

The restaurant is about halfway up the hill, and the road gets a little twisty along the way. Pulling into the car park, I find a spot and come to a stop. I look at Lana. "Ready?"

"Yes. I'm so looking forward to this."

I grin. "Me too."

After opening her car door, I lead her into the restaurant where we're shown to our seats. It's a simple layout with wooden tables and chairs and a polished wooden floor. I also know from looking online it's not too expensive—the last thing I needed was to intimidate Lana with something too pricey.

"Here's the menu. I'll give you a moment to look it over and I'll take your drinks order." The waitress smiles.

"Thank you," I say.

She nods. "You're welcome."

After we've selected drinks and our meals, I knit my fingers together and look across at my date. She's got her head down, and she's fiddling with the knife and fork.

"I get the impression you don't go out much?" I ask.

Lana looks up and shakes her head. "Not really. I left home, got a job, didn't date before Casey, and then she became my life."

"You're amazing."

She drops her gaze. "I'm just living my life. Same as a lot of people."

"Yes, but you're bringing up Casey by yourself, working a full-time job in an awkward situation, and you make it all look so easy."

The drinks arrive, and I take a sip of Heineken. Lana tries her bourbon and Coke. She closes her eyes and smiles with a contented sigh.

"Tough day?" I ask.

Lana fixes her gaze on me. "Not really. I've been nervous all day though. Not sure if drinking this will sooth those nerves or make me embarrass myself. I'm not much of a drinker."

I hold out my palms. "You can't embarrass yourself in front of me. For what it's worth, *I've* been nervous all day too."

She tilts her head. "Why would you be nervous?"

"First date with a beautiful woman. It's scary." I shrug.

She laughs, and it sounds so good.

"It's nice to see you've got a smile on your face. I know this whole thing with Casey must have freaked you out."

Lana takes another sip of her drink before she answers. "It's been a bit of a crazy week."

We talk some more about life, work, and her daughter, and then our meals arrive, interrupting our conversation. I take a taste of the grilled lamb I ordered and nod my approval. "This is good. Not as good as your cooking."

Lana rolls her eyes. "Whatever."

"I mean it. What's yours like?"

She ordered the braised beef cheeks, and I watch, fascinated, as she forks some and raises it to her mouth.

"Are you watching me eat?"

"Not yet."

She chuckles and pops the forkful into her mouth, moaning. "Oh my god, that's so tender."

"I'm glad you said yes to coming out with me."

As she blinks rapidly, her lips quiver. "I ... I'm glad you asked me."

Slicing another piece of lamb, I look at my plate. "Eat up. I've got plans after this."

EATING.

Stealing glances.

Her beautiful smiles.

I knew this night was a good idea. She has no idea just how much I wanted her to say yes, and now she's here with me.

"How's filming going?" she asks.

"Good." I lean back in my seat. "I mean, we really just started. Most of my scenes for the next couple of months are during the day, and then there'll be some night shoots before my part is over. Thankfully, they'll be when the weather should be getting warmer."

She puts down her knife and fork. "How long are you here for?"

"Until November. The shoot is pretty complex, and I'm not in a lead role but I am in a lot of scenes. It's pretty full on."

"November," she says quietly. "About four months?"

I nod. "And then I've got another role I've been waiting to hear back about which I'll be straight into if I get it."

"Where?"

"Back in LA." I draw in a breath. "It's working with Josh Carter and Reece Evans. I've worked hard for the part, but they're taking their sweet time to decide on the casting."

Lana blinks rapidly, and I reach across the table, placing my hand on hers. "Hey. I'm here, and I'm not going anywhere for a while yet."

"I knew you'd leave, but ..."

"If you're not happy about me leaving, I know I'm right about whatever this is between us."

Her lips twitch, and she drops her gaze. "I thought that was obvious given Casey's never had a babysitter before."

I shuffle my chair around the table until I'm sitting next to her. "That means a lot to me. I hope you know that."

She flutters her eyelashes—I'm not even sure she's aware she's doing it.

"Let's get out of here."

Her lips twitch. "Where are we going?"

I stand and hold out my hand. "Why don't we drive the rest of the way up the peak? It's a clear night, and I've not been there yet."

Lana takes my outstretched hand. "It's lovely up there."

"Let's go. You're not too cold, are you?"

She shakes her head. "It'll be fine in the car."

"Come on."

I pay the bill on the way out and open the car door for Lana. Her hand brushes my arm as she steps in and she pauses, looking up at me. I'm going to win this woman's heart if it's the last thing I do.

Getting into the driver's side, I slide the key into the ignition. "You know, the hardest part about being here is this whole 'driving on the wrong side of the road thing'."

She shoots me a bemused look. "It's not the wrong side."

"It is to me." I shrug, start the car, and back out of the parking space.

Peak House is about halfway up the hill, and the road gets narrower and windier as we approach the top. But it's worth the effort.

We picked the right night to come up here.

Tomorrow will be a frosty morning—it's that cold. But it means the night sky is clear. Below us are the street lights of Havelock North, and beyond that, the Hastings glow. Above us, so many stars twinkle. It all combines for a stunning sight.

I look at Lana. She's got a small smile on her face as her eyes scan the scenery.

"Great view," she says.

"Yes. Yes, it is."

She turns her head and grins. "Not me."

"Yes, you. I guess the lights of the city are okay too."

"Thank you for tonight." Her eyes glisten with happiness.

"I'd like to do it again."

Lana bites her bottom lip. "So would I." She holds up her palms. "But we might have to include Casey because I don't want to impose on Maria too often."

"That's fine. She goes to bed early."

Lana's lips curl into a smile. "She does."

"What do you usually do in the evenings once she's asleep?" The thought of her being at home alone saddens me. My mom usually had friends who she spent time with, and they'd take turns at babysitting me. She found her village—I'm not sure Lana has one.

"Sometimes I watch TV. I also read a lot, and I draw."

"Draw?"

She tilts her head. "I used to draw pictures of sheep and cows and landscapes on the farm. Now, it's mostly pictures of Casey."

"I'd love to see them."

"Maybe."

The way she drops her gaze is frustrating. This Gareth guy really did a number on her—and on top of that, she doesn't seem to be confident in her own abilities. I know that feeling. When I first started acting, I had no real idea if I was any good. Encouragement from my mom helped give me the confidence in my ability.

"I haven't seen any of your movies. I'll have to fix that," she says.

I shrug. "I've only made a handful of movies. They did okay at the box office, but nothing too crazy."

"Anna knew who you were. And you were in the magazine Casey found you in."

I chuckle. "My first role was on a daytime soap opera. That's what tends to follow me around. Even though it was for six months three years ago. It got me noticed, though."

Her eyes widen. "Really? Which show was it? We weren't allowed to watch TV when I was a kid, but my mum sure did."

"*Once in a Lifetime.*"

She grips my arm. "I'm pretty sure that's what my mother watched. We saw glimpses of it, but we were never allowed to watch TV for ourselves."

"Not at all?"

Lana shakes her head. "When I said my parents were strict ... we lived on a farm and were home-schooled. The only thing I learned about the world was from books."

"Wow." I frown. "I mean, that's a bit extreme."

She leans her head back on the headrest. "All it meant was by the time I'd finished my schooling, and I was old enough to leave, that I wanted out. I'd learned about the world, but I'd never really gotten to see any of it. Except in books. I didn't get that far in the end."

"What do you mean?"

Lana turns her head and meets my gaze. "I told my parents I wanted to move. They weren't happy, but they understood. And they helped me at first while I found a job and found my feet."

"And that job was with Gareth."

She nods. "I went home one weekend and told my mother everything. But my father ..."

"Shit. I'm so sorry."

Lana shrugs. "Mum sided with him. She always did. I was a bad influence on my younger sisters, and they didn't want me to visit anymore. I was on my own." She swallows hard. "You know the rest of the story."

My head spins. I don't understand it in the slightest. My mother was a lot of things, but she'd never have abandoned me like that.

"Have I scared you off yet?" she says softly.

I shake my head. "No, angel. If anything, it makes me feel even more protective of you and Casey. The two of you need me."

She laughs. "You think so, huh?"

"I know so." I lean closer. "I really want to kiss you right now."

Her breath hitches. "Maybe you should."

I love the way her nose twitches as she waits for me to make the next move, and then her tongue darts out to wet her lips.

There's no way I can keep her waiting.

I'm way too much of a gentleman for that.

We start out soft and slow, my lips pressing against hers before she opens up to me. Her mouth is sweet with the slight hint of cola, and her shoulders relax as I probe her mouth with my tongue.

This isn't just a kiss. It's the two of us connecting on a whole new level—one she's not experienced with. Hell, I've had a single serious relationship with a few shorter ones. But I'm the one who'll have to guide her through this.

And it's hot as hell.

She lets out the smallest of sighs against my mouth, and I end the kiss, pressing my nose to hers.

"Alex," she whispers.

"I'm right here." I pull back a little to look at her.

She raises her hands to cup my face. "Thank you."

"For what?"

"Tonight has been perfect."

I brush my lips against hers. "You're about to tell me it's time to go home."

She laughs softly. "Well, it is the first time I've been out for the evening without Casey."

I nod, reaching up for her hands and taking them in mine. After pressing a kiss to one of her palms, I let them go. "I'm sure she's missing you as much as you're missing her."

"I'm sorry ..."

I cock my head. "I'm not. I know how close you two are. I'm a big disruption."

"A nice one." She grins. "And one I want more of."

"Let's get you home to Casey." I tug on my seat belt, and turn the key in the ignition.

Lana reaches across and places her hand on my arm. "I hope you know I don't want this night to end. But I also want to get home to her."

"It's okay. I understand." I put the car into gear. "When my mom started dating when I was a boy, there were nights she'd be out late, and other nights when she'd come home early and we'd watch a movie with a bowl of popcorn."

She folds her hands in her lap. "I think I'd like your mother. I love those kind of nights with Casey."

Our drive home is quiet, and it's over seemingly in a flash as we pull up outside her flat. I get out the car and open her door. She takes my hand and doesn't let go while I lock the car.

"I'll walk you inside. You know, make sure you get there okay."

Lana loops her arm in mine. "We just have to make sure Casey doesn't find out you're here. She might not let you leave."

"That wouldn't be *that* bad."

"I'm so not ready for that."

I stop, and she pauses beside me. "I'm sorry, I didn't mean ..." I say.

"I wasn't making assumptions. It's just that I don't want to rush anything." She looks at her feet. "I probably just worded that badly."

Nudging her shoulder with mine, I take a step. "No. I already worked out that you need to take this slow. And I'm fine with that."

"I'm glad," she says. We walk slowly until we reach the door. "I've really enjoyed tonight. Do you want to come in for a coffee?"

I nod. "I'd like that."

She pushes open the door. Maria's seated on the couch, and she stands to greet us.

"You're home early."

Lana smiles. "I missed Casey."

She laughs. "She's fast asleep. She wanted desperately to stay up and see you when you got home. But she curled up on the couch next to me, and we watched some cartoons until she nodded off."

"Thank you again. I'm so glad she had you. She just loves spending time with you at day care."

"I love being her teacher." She nods toward me. "Goodnight to both of you. I hope you had a good time."

"We did." Lana takes my hand and squeezes it.

"Good. See you on Monday morning." Maria picks up her bag and jacket, and we step aside to let her out the door.

"I'll walk you to your car," I say.

She smiles. "No. You stay here where it's warm. It's just outside."

"Are you sure?"

Maria shifts her gaze to Lana. "Oh, this one is a keeper."

Lana raises her hand to her mouth and laughs.

"Bye." Maria waves and closes the door as she leaves.

I turn to Lana. "So ... alone again."

Her eyes glisten with happiness. "Looks like it. Casey used to be the worst sleeper, and get up what felt like fifty times in a night, but the past few months, she's been solid."

"Oh. So, there's not much chance of us being interrupted?" I raise my hand to her cheek, brushing a stray strand of hair behind her ear.

"Not really. What should we do?"

"I'd really like to kiss you again."

A smile dances on her lips. "I wouldn't say no."

I lean in.

"Mummy," Casey calls.

Lana covers her eyes with her hand and shakes her head. "So much for that."

"Better make it quick, then."

She drops her hand. "What?"

I kiss her, and she laughs into my mouth, which just makes me smile.

"Did you just waste a kiss, Ms Maitland?" I ask.

"I believe I did. Might have to get one some other time to make up for it."

I scan her expression. Her face is flush with excitement, her eyes dancing.

"Did you just ask me out again?" I ask.

She shoves my shoulder. "I think I did. You should get out of here before Casey sees you or you'll never be allowed to leave."

"Again—would that really be so bad?" I shrug, my palms up.

"Stop it." She laughs softly.

"I will call you tomorrow. And probably the day after that. And …"

Her smile grows. "I get the picture."

"Good. Because I plan on seeing you again. Whether alone or with Casey." I reach for her hand. "Goodnight, angel."

"Goodnight," she whispers.

I peck her on the cheek and step out of the flat, closing the door behind me. It takes everything in me not to skip back to the car.

Tonight was everything I'd hoped it would be and more. It's not going to be easy to pursue a romance while I'm working, but I'm determined to put in the effort.

Lana Maitland is worth it.

8

LANA

On Monday, I'm still floating.

Alex texted me yesterday to tell me he was thinking about me, and he's all I've been able to think about.

He made me feel more special than I've felt in a long time.

It's nothing like the way things were between Gareth and me. No secrets and no lies. There's no wife he's not telling me about, and, thanks to Anna, I've brushed up on my Alex Stone general knowledge.

He likes me for me.

Gareth always told me we couldn't go out in public because people would judge our age gap. While that was probably true, it turned out to just be that he was married. Alex has already taken me out once.

And he was right—no one seemed to recognise him.

I'm on automatic pilot all morning, getting through my work without any interruptions. Close to lunch, the door opens, and I'm not paying attention until Anna approaches me.

"Lana, this is for you."

Anna places a bouquet of red roses and a gift basket on my desk.

My eyebrows take on a life of their own as they rise, and I grin as I pick up a baked item from the basket and take a sniff.

Banana muffin.

"Those flowers are so beautiful. Now you *have* to spill all the goss about your date."

I take a bite of the muffin. "Mm-hmm well …"

She shakes her head. "I'll take the basket away if you're going to hold out on me."

I swallow and laugh. "It was really lovely. He's just such a nice guy."

"Good. You deserve a nice guy." She flounces back to her chair and drops onto it. "I was really scared that you'd tell me I was the fan of a douche."

"He's not that at all." I smile. "He's very sweet. Want one of these? I can't eat them all. I'll take a couple home for Casey, but I think there's about a dozen in there."

Anna leans over and plucks one out of the basket. "Yes, I will have one of these delicious banana muffins your Hollywood star boyfriend gave you."

I laugh. "He's not my boyfriend."

She wags a finger. "We're not doing that again. Besides, he obviously likes you. Look at all this." Taking a bite of the muffin, she lets out a loud moan. "Ohhh, that is so good."

"What on earth is with all the moaning going on out here?" Gareth steps out of his office, and both Anna and I burst into giggles.

I hold up the basket. "Want a muffin?"

He eyes me cautiously. "What's wrong with them?"

"Nothing. They're amazing. And I'll never eat all these by myself."

Anna points at the basket. "Try one, Gareth. They're freshly baked."

He reaches for one and sniffs at it before taking a bite. "Where did these come from?" he asks.

"Alex sent them to Lana. It's so sweet." I swear Anna has love hearts in her eyes as she says the words.

Gareth's eyebrows rise. "Is that right?"

"Yes." I let out a contented sigh. "I don't know how he got this so right, but he nailed it."

"You didn't read the card," Anna says.

I laugh. "I think the smell of those muffins overrode any thought I had about that."

She pulls the envelope off the flowers and hands it to me.

Thank you for a great night. I need to see you again.

The thought of him doing this makes my heart flutter.

I blush and tuck the card back into the envelope.

"What did it say?" Anna asks.

I shrug. "He wants to see me again."

She lets out a squeal and Gareth narrows his gaze. "So, are you going to?"

"Are you kidding?" I reach for another muffin. "This is *so* the way to my heart. I just have to remember to keep some for Casey to eat."

He rolls his eyes and makes his way back into his office.

Nothing can get me down.

Not even working for *him*.

9

ALEX

wo weeks.

It's been two weeks since that first date, and I can't stop thinking about Lana.

I haven't managed to coax her out of the house again, but I've had dinner at her place a few times, and other times I've visited after Casey's gone to bed. Things are going fast emotionally, but slow physically—we haven't progressed past kissing and caressing, but I'm content to let things move at Lana's pace.

She's worth it.

"Hey, Alex. Got a minute?"

I look up as Peter, one of the security guards, jogs toward me.

"Sure." The crew and staff of the production are here even when the weather's shitty and miserable, and Peter's one of those people who has a smile on his face no matter what. I've always got a minute for him.

"You've got visitors at the main gate."

"I do?"

He beams. "Reece Evans."

My stomach falls to my feet. "You're kidding."

He shakes his head. "Nope. He's here with my cousin Pania. Apparently, she's his girlfriend."

I laugh. "Wow. Small world."

Peter just keeps on shaking his head. "Aotearoa can be like that. Come on, I'll walk you to them."

It's not a long walk, but the whole time my heart beats about a million times a second. Reece can't be here with bad news, can he? Just him being here is incredible. I've wanted to work with him forever—especially after the way he and Josh Carter cleaned up the Oscars with their movie.

If there were anyone's career in Hollywood I wanted to emulate, it'd be one of those two.

As I round a corner and reach the fence, there he is, large as life on the other side of it.

At the audition, the casting director remarked that we could pass as brothers, but seeing him up close like this only drives that idea home. He's older than me, and slightly taller, and if he's here to give me the news I hope he is—we'll be brothers on-screen soon.

The gate opens.

"Reece Evans. What are you doing here?" *Please say you're here to offer me the role.*

He grins. "I've come to offer you a job."

I hold out my hand and hope he doesn't notice it's trembling. This is crazy. I'm having a fan moment in front of the man I hope to be working with next.

Settle down.

"Really? You came all the way here to do that?"

Reece laughs. "I was here for other reasons, but Josh thought it'd be something special for me to deliver the news in person."

I nod, trying to control the action and not overdo it. "Sounds great. Have you spoken to my agent? I haven't heard anything from him yet."

Reece holds up his palms. "Josh is handling all that. I'm guessing no, or maybe he's told them I'm delivering the news personally. But we're not really good at doing things the traditional way."

I laugh. "So I hear. I look forward to working with you guys."

He cocks his head. "You want the role?"

Shit.

I didn't even say yes.

"Does a bear shit in the woods? Hell yes, I want it. The chance to work with you and Josh Carter after your Oscar clean-up is mind-boggling. I'd be an idiot to say no."

"Ahem."

I've been so focused on Reece, I barely noticed the woman standing beside him who smiles at me as I shift my gaze to her.

Reece shuffles his feet. "Oh, Alex. This is my girlfriend, Pania. Pania, my future co-star Alex Stone."

Pania smiles and takes my outstretched hand to shake it. Reece raises his eyebrows at her.

"What? He's cute," she says.

I grin. "I like her."

"Don't like her too much. I just got her," he says.

Pania and I laugh.

"We should have dinner or something to celebrate. Have you got some time?" Reece asks.

I look back over my shoulder. I've got another scene to shoot, but that's not for a couple of hours. "I should be finished up here around four I think. It depends, though. You know how things go."

He nods. "How about I give you my number, and you text me when you're ready? And bring your partner if you have one. We're not in a hurry to leave town." He reaches for Pania's hand and kisses it. "We can stay another night."

Pania beams. "I like that idea."

Watching them makes me think of Lana. I'm not sure if she

can find a babysitter at short notice, but I'll have to call and ask her. She'll be so excited—she knows how much this role means to me. This could be everything for me.

"Sounds good. Things have gone pretty well today. I think we should be good."

"Great," Reece says.

He gives me his number before we shake hands again and say goodbye.

I don't care about calling my agent—that can wait.

There's only one person I want to call with this news.

"ALEX? IS EVERYTHING OKAY?" Her tone is cautious when I call her. I've never called her like this in the middle of the day.

"Oh, babe. More than okay. I have some amazing news."

She's breathless. "You got the part?"

"How did you guess?" I laugh.

"Oh. Only because you've been going on and on about it. Am I right?"

My chest swells. I'm so proud. "Yes. I got it."

"I knew you would."

Clutching my phone to my ear, I raise my face to the sky and whisper a *thank you.* "You have a lot of faith in me."

"Well, I'm not sure how I've done it, but I scored this amazing guy who also happens to be an incredible actor."

I chew on my bottom lip before I hit her with the next part. "Reece Evans delivered the news personally."

"Oh, no way."

"Yeah. So, he's asked me out to dinner tonight. He's here with his girlfriend."

"Reece Evans has a girlfriend?"

I chuckle. "Yes. Her name's Pania. Anyway, I'm calling to see if you want to come with me."

There's silence for a moment.

"Lana, it's okay if you can't. I know getting a babysitter is difficult, especially at late notice. And if you can't come, I'll drop by your place afterward to see you."

"I'd like that." Her voice is breathy. I'm so crazy about this woman, and I want her—really want her. We're so close to taking that next step, and there are times when it's all I think about.

She's who I want to share this moment with.

For now, I have one more phone call to make.

Mom takes a while to answer—she always does. I'm not even exactly sure where she is right now. A while ago she cashed in everything she had and started travelling. So far, she's not left the US, but there seems to be a lot she wants to see in our country before going overseas.

I'm not sure where she'll live or what she'll do when she runs out of money. But my mom is like a cat and has more than one life, I'm sure.

"Alex. It's so good to hear from you. Are you in New Zealand? What's it like? Are they feeding you properly?"

All that before I can catch my breath to speak.

Mom has boundless energy. She'd have been a hippy if we'd lived in the seventies, with her lust for life and carefree attitude. I'm the responsible one out of the two of us.

"I am, Mom. And it's amazing. I'm calling to let you know I got that part I wanted."

"The one in the Reece Evans film?"

I'm not sure what it is, but from the moment I told her I'd auditioned and how badly I wanted the role, she's called it that. I think she's got a crush on him, which is awkward to think about, but typical of Mom.

"Yes. This is it, Mom. This could be my big break."

"Oh, Alex. I'm so proud of you."

"I know."

Mom was the one who encouraged me to pursue acting. She knew I wanted to, but I'd held back because I thought I had to be the one who went out to support us—and acting wasn't going to do that.

Or so I'd thought at the start.

But she signed me up for acting classes, and then encouraged me to audition for a TV show which I did six months of before moving into movies. I'm no household name, but if my mom had anything to do with it, I would be.

"Anyway, I just wanted to give you a call and let you know. I haven't even spoken to my agent yet," I say.

"Well, congratulations." She sighs. "And you get to work with Reece Evans. That will be wonderful."

I roll my eyes and shake my head. "I'm sure it will be. Love you, Mom."

"Love you too."

No sooner do I disconnect the call with my mom than my agent calls.

"Charlie. I guess you heard the news?"

He laughs. "I know you had some visitors to set. How do you feel?"

"Over the moon."

"Good. I think you'll be more than happy with the offer they made. I'll send it through to you and you can let me know how you feel."

I snicker. "You know I already told him yes."

"I figured as much. And you're right to do so. This is going to put your career on the map. Congratulations."

"Thanks ..." I look up to see one of the assistants waving at me. "I've gotta go. But I'm looking forward to seeing that offer in writing."

"You bet. Talk later."

I take a deep breath before turning and heading back toward the set. It'll be hard to focus on anything this afternoon, and I can't wait for dinner tonight.

I ARRIVE at the restaurant early.

It's just as well, because I could do with a drink at the bar first to steady my nerves. I'm tired after my early start, but wide awake because tonight I get to spend time with one of my idols.

And then with Lana.

I'm not working tomorrow, which is just as well because after all this excitement, I'm sure to crash. But it's all worth it.

I sip slowly at my drink. I'll have this and one more at dinner and call that a night, given that I have plans with my girl later.

Today's news changes everything.

It gives me hope for the future. Not just for my career, but for my personal life. Lana manages because she's stuck in this job with her ex, but what if I could help? What if I could make a difference?

Finishing my drink, I ask to be seated at our table and wait.

It's not long before I see the familiar figure of Reece Evans approaching.

Now, people look.

He's got such a presence that heads are turning, and I can see there are at least a couple of starstruck expressions on faces around the room.

At first, everything's a bit of a haze as he shakes my hand and takes a seat at the table. Pania orders wine, but I'm barely paying attention.

"Good day?" he asks.

"Long day." I lean back. "I was in makeup at three this morning, but we wanted to shoot the dawn, and we did, so it was worth it."

"Great."

The wine arrives, and Reece holds up his glass. "To Alex. Congratulations on joining our team."

A lump appears in my throat. I can't quite believe this. Getting this role and working with people the calibre of Reece and Josh Carter is something I thought I'd only dream of.

"To Alex." Pania holds up her glass. She has no idea she just saved me from being completely unable to speak, and I nod toward both of them.

I'm about to get everything I dreamed of and more.

And I can't wait to see Lana.

ONCE I'M in the door, Lana's in my arms in an instant, and I'm lost in her soft scent and her gentle touch.

"I'm glad you're here. Congratulations," she says.

I press my forehead to hers. "That means a lot coming from you."

"How did your dinner go?"

I take her hand and lead her to the couch where we sit. "Amazing, but I'm really happy to be with you now."

"I'm so proud of you, Alex. Stay with me tonight?" Her eyes search mine.

This is big for her. She hasn't trusted a man since Gareth, and what a monumental waste of time he turned out to be. I won't let her down. Lana means way too much to me for that.

I cup her cheek. "Are you sure? I want you to be certain that this is what you want."

"It is. I want to be with you."

"I want that too."

Lana drops her gaze. "There's just one thing."

I scan her expression. Whatever it is, she's nervous about saying it. I can tell by the way she blinks rapidly and from her accelerated breathing. She's grown in confidence since we've been together, but there are times where she's still unsure of herself. One of those times shouldn't be when we're about to be intimate.

"Anything."

She snags her bottom lip with her teeth, and my cock twitches.

"I don't want Casey to know about this yet. Not us. I mean, she knows we're spending time together, but staying the night is next level."

I take her hand in mine. "I have to leave early to get to set anyway. Is Casey likely to wake up?"

She shakes her head. "Not until about six."

"Good."

Her eyebrows rise.

"The things I want to do with you? There's no way I want her to see."

Lana giggles, and it's the most beautiful sound in the world. I'm sure there hasn't been a lot of laughter for her in the past few years, and now I have it all.

Pulling her to her feet, I take a step toward the hallway.

"Alex, there's something else."

I turn back. "What is it?"

"I'm not ..." Her voice trails off, and I tilt my head.

"I know you're not a virgin, if that's what you're trying to say."

She claps her hand over her mouth and giggles. "That much is obvious." Making her laugh seems to bring out her confidence again. "I don't have much in the way of experience."

I shrug. "We can make up for that. I think I have just enough."

"Just enough for what?"

I lean in, our faces inches apart. "Enough to make you very happy."

"I'm already happy," she whispers.

She squeals when I scoop her into my arms. "Extra happy. Happier than you've ever been in your life. Screamingly happy."

Lana laughs. "Is that even a word?"

"It is now. Your bedroom is down the end of the hall, yes?"

She buries her face in my neck. "That's right."

I carry her to the end of the hallway and into her room. It's not a large room, but it has a queen-size bed which will do just fine.

"Alex," she whispers. "Close the door."

I lower her gently onto the mattress and turn back to close the door. As I return to the bed, she watches me—anticipation all over her face. Her chest rises and falls rapidly as I approach, and I tug my T-shirt over my head and lie down onto the bed beside her.

"We go as fast as you're comfortable with, okay? Tell me if you want to stop."

She nods, then runs a hand down my chest.

I grab her hand and press a kiss to her fingertips. After reaching for the hem of her shirt, I pull it up while she sits up to make it easier.

While I drop her shirt to the floor, she unclips her bra and lies back down.

Her breasts are small, but enough to fill my hands, and her nipples spring to life as I stroke one and then the other, marvelling in her body.

"Alex."

I smile as her blush extends from her cheeks all the way to her collarbone. "Lana."

"Stop looking at me like that. It's embarrassing." She laughs softly.

"You're just so beautiful."

Her eyelashes flutter. I doubt she's used to compliments, but I'm not about to stop.

I unbutton her jeans. Her eyes follow every move I make, and I meet her gaze as I slide the zip down. She raises her hips so I can get her out of them, leaving her in just her panties.

"I want to see you," she whispers.

Slipping off the bed, I drop my jeans to the floor, followed by my boxers. She sucks in a breath. Touching her has left me hard as a rock.

"Alex," she whispers.

I love that. I love my name on her lips. Now I want to hear her call it out as I give her all the pleasure I can. I plan on taking my angel to heaven.

Slipping back into bed beside her, I stroke her thighs with one hand while flicking my tongue over a nipple. Her body tenses.

"It's okay, Lana. Just relax."

She laughs softly. "It's been a while."

"I know. I won't hurt you."

Her brows knit. "I wouldn't let you in here if I thought you would."

"Good." I raise my hand to run my index finger down her cheek. "Now let me touch you."

She lets out a contented sigh as I brush my fingertips down her body and between her legs. Parting them a little, I slide a finger into her. She lets out a tiny gasp.

"I've been thinking about this ever since we met," I whisper. "I know we had other distractions that day, but you were ... are the most beautiful woman I've ever seen."

She cups my cheek. "You sweet talker."

"And now you're mine." I slide my finger back out of her and over her clit. She catches her bottom lip between her teeth.

She rocks against my finger, and I slow, letting her do whatever she needs to get off. I claim her mouth with mine, my tongue in rhythm with my finger.

"Alex. Alex, please." She pants, and I take in her needy expression.

Lana deserves the very best of me.

And I'll be damned if I'm holding back.

"Tell me what you want, angel," I whisper.

"I don't know."

"Do you want to come?"

"I ... I ..." Her eyelids seem heavy as she fights against closing them.

"Just let it happen, angel. Just relax into me."

She grips my arm, closes her eyes, and lets out a long breath. And then there's a moment where it feels like nothing's happening. My fingers work her clit. Her body tenses.

Lana lets out a moan, and shudders beneath my hand. Her fingernails bite into my skin and I watch, entranced as she bites her bottom lip, eyes still closed.

I ease up the pressure, and her eyelids flicker open.

"Was that ...?"

'Don't tell me you've never come before."

Her expression's so blank it stabs me inside. I already disliked Gareth without knowing him because of the way he'd treated her. Now it makes me even more angry to realise he really did put himself first.

"I thought I had." Her cheeks are flushed, and I don't even know if it's from exertion or embarrassment. "But that was nothing like ..."

"Did you enjoy it?"

She gets this faraway look in her eyes, and I don't need her to answer.

"Yes. Oh yes." Lana shoots a glance sideways. "There are condoms in the top drawer of the bedside cabinet."

"You know I'm not finished yet—not by a long shot."

Her lips twitch into a smile. "I'm ready."

"Spread your legs for me."

She parts her legs, and I move between them. Lana's probably the first woman I've been with who doesn't shave or wax, but that light blonde hair is barely there, and it suits her.

"Alex?" Her voice quivers.

I lean over.

She trembles as I place a kiss on each inner thigh, working my way up. If I didn't know she'd been celibate for so long, I wouldn't be so patient, but it's been so long for Lana. I want her to savour every touch, every kiss.

I want them burned into her brain to erase all the bad shit that's been done to her in the past—so her memories are good and of me.

"Ooooh." She arches her back when I lick her clit.

Grinning, I go to town as she wriggles against me. I look up after she moans in time to see her stuff her hand against her mouth.

And then I get back to enjoying her scent, and her taste, and I want to proclaim that it's mine and mine alone.

All of it.

My need for her only grows the more we share.

She comes again, against my face, and I can't wait any longer.

"Are you okay?" I ask.

Her eyes are hazed over, and her smile lights a fire in me that I never want extinguished. "Oh, yes."

I open the drawer and pull out a box of condoms, then take one out. She studies me closely as I open it and roll the condom down my cock.

"Yes. Oh, yes," she says.

There's no way I'm waiting after that. But I can't lose control too quickly. I want this moment to last as long as possible.

I thrust inside her.

She grasps my shoulders, pulling me down to kiss her.

"Still okay?" I ask.

"So much better than okay," she whispers.

We move in sync, and she lets out a shaky breath with each thrust.

"Ride me." I flip onto my back, pulling her with me, and she laughs softly, pressing her hands against my chest.

Gripping her thighs, I slide the rest of the way back in again. "You feel so fucking good," I say.

She rocks her hips, grinding against me, and I blow out a breath in an effort to last just that little bit longer.

But it's tough. She's so tight and hot around me, and I can't stop when she straightens up and rolls against me.

"Lana." I let out a cry, losing all control as I come. It's not enough though. I want this all the time—I want her in my bed every night.

She comes to a stop. Her eyes are closed, her lips parted, a blissful look all over her face.

I still. Slowly, she opens her eyes.

"Are you still with me, angel?" I ask.

Lana's lazy smile fills my heart with joy. It's the smile of a sated woman, and I did that. I put that smile on her face.

She slides off me and rolls onto her back. "I didn't know it could be that good."

"Well, now you do."

"I'm so tired."

"You're not the only one." I laugh and point at the condom. "I should get rid of this."

"There's a bin in the bathroom."

She lies back and closes her eyes while I dispose of it and come back. As I get into bed she sits up.

"I'll be back in a minute."

When she returns, I pull her into my arms, her back against my chest, and nuzzle her neck.

"I think I'm going to sleep like a log now," she murmurs.

And then there are no more words because her breathing evens out as she drops off to sleep.

I close my eyes and draw in a deep breath.

This isn't what I came to this country for, but now I'm doubly grateful for being cast. The movie will be a boost for my career, but this? This is the best thing that's ever happened to me. *She* is the best thing that's ever happened to me.

Lana is the unexpected bonus, and this is far more than a fling as far as I'm concerned.

She's my future.

10

———————

LANA

Before I know it, it's like we're a family.

No.

Alex's acceptance of Casey calling him Daddy made it easy. Maybe too easy.

I've protected us both from heartache all this time, not letting anyone get too close. But I made an exception because Casey practically demanded it. And now I worry we're all in too deep.

Casey knows Alex isn't her father, but she still calls him Daddy. And me? I'm falling in love with this man who sends me a basket of banana muffins and my favourite flowers once a week at work.

But his time here is going to come to an end—and soon.

It's hard to think about that when I'm curled up in bed with his warm body beside me. We've continued to keep this part of our relationship a secret from Casey. Getting to know him is one thing. Finding him in my bed is another.

"I should go," Alex murmurs. "I've got to get to set, and Casey will be awake soon."

I nod, clasping my hands above my head and stretching. "You should."

Before I know it, his lips are on my nipple, and I laugh as a warm hand cups my other breast.

"This is the life." I sigh.

"I could do this every day with you," he says.

I laugh softly. "You nearly are. If neither of us had to work …"

"We'd never get out of bed." His kisses are tender and gentle. I've never had a relationship like this—nothing compares to it. Letting go will be one of the hardest things I've ever had to do.

But I can see a time when I'll have to do it.

Thinking is hard, though, when Alex kisses his way down my body, positioning himself between my legs with a sly grin on his face.

Oh, how I love this part.

He places gentle kisses on each thigh, and I grip the headboard, wiggling toward him.

"That's my girl," he murmurs.

I let out a moan as his tongue brushes my clit.

The door flies open.

"Mummy. Why the door closed?"

I freeze, and Alex's hot breath hits me as laughter comes from under the covers. I bite my bottom lip.

"Daddy? What you doing under there?"

I face-palm, and it's so hard not to laugh.

Alex doesn't miss a beat. "I'm hiding so I can surprise you, silly." He climbs up the bed and pulls the cover back over his head. "Peekaboo."

Casey shakes her head. "I not a baby."

"No, sweetheart. You are not." He chuckles.

"Mummy, can we have breakfast?" she asks.

I check the bedside clock and groan. "Casey, honey. It's five in the morning. Way too early."

"I'll make some breakfast." Alex pulls himself up so he's sitting next to me. "What are we eating?"

I press my lips together to stop from laughing.

"Mummy makes me toast. Do you want toast, Daddy?"

"I'll come and make you some toast in a minute. Why don't you go and turn the TV on?" I say.

"I can watch TV?"

I pinch the bridge of my nose. She's never allowed to watch TV before we go to day care. The one and only time I ever let her, she had a tantrum when we had to leave because she wanted to finish the show she was watching.

"Just this once," I reply.

She runs from the room, and the unmistakeable theme tune of Paw Patrol floats back through the air.

I cover my eyes and let go of the laughter. "Good recovery."

Alex nuzzles my neck. "I thought so. We're probably lucky she hasn't caught us before this."

"I know, but ..." I laugh again. "So awkward."

"She's fine. But I do have to get going after I make her breakfast. You were distracting me."

I widen my eyes. "Me? You were keeping yourself quite entertained there."

"I wasn't the only one." He kisses me softly. "How about ..." He runs a finger down my breast. "... I come by this evening and we get some takeout and just hang out. I'll help you if you need it with Casey, and then you and me can have the whole Friday night together."

"Are you real?"

He kisses my fingertips. "I am. And for what it's worth, I'm glad I was accosted by a three-year-old in the park because it led me to her mother. Who is the sweetest, most loving, gentle person I've ever met."

"You're pretty nice yourself."

"I want more, Lana. I want it all with you."

I swallow hard. "We should go and sort out this toast."

"Lana," he says, grasping my hand. "I think I'm falling in love with you."

My heart thuds. I was sure that there was no future in this. How could there be? When his movie's over, he'll leave the country again and all that'll be left is the memory of the nights we spent together.

Not this.

I never thought it would go this far.

"I'm sure you think that, but—"

"I know how I feel. I don't want us to just be a short-term thing."

My lips tremble as I rack my brain to think of what to say. "Can we talk about this later?"

He nods. "I know Casey's waiting. And I know it's a lot to deal with at five in the morning. I just wanted you to know how I feel."

I rub the back of my neck, still unsure what to say. I've fought my deeper feelings for him, but it seems he feels the same way. But I can't focus on that right now.

"Mummy. Daddy," Casey yells from the living room.

"Let's go." He smiles, and warmth spreads through my chest. I want this. I want to wake up in the mornings next to him and be there on his journey. I'm not sure how I can do that from New Zealand, but I want more too.

Maybe this doesn't have to end.

I'm out of bed first, slipping on a T-shirt and grabbing my bathrobe on the way out the door.

Casey's standing in front of the television, eyes glued to it. This is such a bad idea, but I don't even care this morning.

After placing some slices of bread in the toaster, I put the kettle on. There's no point making Casey breakfast and going back to bed. I might as well make coffee and be thankful yet again that it's Friday.

After a couple of minutes the toast pops up, and I scrape some butter and Marmite onto it before taking it out to Casey.

Alex emerges from the hallway, smelling of my vanilla bodywash. He scratches his neck as he walks out.

"Daddy, I got toast," Casey says.

"So you do." Alex reaches me and pecks me on the cheek. "I'll grab some breakfast on set. I'll let you know later what time I'll come over."

"It's a deal." I kiss his lips. "Maybe then you can finish what you started half an hour ago."

His grin is way too cheerful for this time of the day. "Now *that's* a deal."

He ruffles Casey's hair on the way out and then disappears into the early morning. This feels so normal, it's difficult to believe. He's off to work while we start our day.

"Daddy go to work?" Casey asks.

I'm distracted as I watch the door Alex went through.

He said he's falling in love with me.

I'm falling in love with him too.

It's the longest day ever as I mull over what Alex said this morning.

He wants more.

I guess I knew this was coming from the way things have been going. Didn't I?

I want more too.

I'm not sure how this will work given he'll leave the country once his movie's finished. Can we have a relationship long-distance? Or will it fizzle out? Am I overthinking things?

Alex: *I won't be out of here until after around seven. Want me to bring dinner over?*

I let out a long breath, reading his text. That's Alex to a tee. He's had a long day, but still thinking of making my life easier.

Me: *Sounds good. I'll feed Casey. Maybe she'll fall asleep early.*

Alex: *Are you propositioning me?*

I laugh out loud. Anna turns her head and arches an eyebrow at me, but I shrug and go back to my phone.

Me: *Maybe*

Alex: *Can't wait*

"How's it going with Alex Stone?" Anna asks.

I look up. "Uhh, good."

"I still can't believe you're dating him. He's gorgeous." Her eyes widen and she slams her hand over her mouth. "I didn't mean that the way it came out. You two look so good together."

Laughing, I put my phone back on the desk. "It's okay. I knew what you meant."

"What's he like?"

I say nothing at first, but she rolls her eyes.

"Oh, you don't even have to say anything," she says.

"What?"

"The grin on your face says it all. That good, huh? Does he have any friends he can introduce me to?"

I lean back in my seat. "I can ask him."

She sighs. "I liked that Reece Evans, and he was apparently in New Zealand not long ago. But he's got a girlfriend, I hear."

If she's fishing for information, I'm not about to tell her I know the answer to that. Do people talk like this about Alex? My stomach churns at the thought. "I don't really follow movie stars that much."

"Whatever." She laughs. "You knew who Alex Stone was before you met him, didn't you?"

I screw up my face. "Well, yes, but only from magazines. I hadn't actually seen him in anything."

Her mouth falls open. "What?"

"When I was at home, my parents wouldn't let us watch much in the way of television, and then I had a baby who wouldn't sleep. Other priorities, I guess."

She cocks her head. "I never thought about that. You have social media though, right?"

I nod. "Of course." If you count the Facebook account where I have a handful of mothers from day care as friends. My sisters have nothing like that back home, and while I miss them, they're not likely to pop up on social media any time soon unless they make the break like I did. It might happen eventually, but as for when? Who knows?

"So, you must have seen trailers? Or teasers for shows and movies?"

"Of course." And that's true. But I read a lot when Casey's asleep and that's my entertainment. My life hasn't really lent itself to much more than that. It's what happens when you're alone and you fall pregnant.

"Well, he's been in quite a few things. Though nothing like this movie, and I hear he's up for a part opposite Reece Evans."

I draw in a sharp breath. "I don't know a lot about his work. He's just Alex." Alex hasn't asked me not to say anything, but the last thing I want to do is put his work at risk.

She smiles. "That is so cute. Make sure you ask him about his friends."

"Sure."

IN THE EARLY EVENING, Casey sits at the coffee table, a sausage in one hand, her eyes glued to the television. Her upbringing is so different to mine, and I'm glad for it. She'll be able to dream big and go for it, and I'll be right behind her.

The sheltered life I lived is so far behind me, and I don't miss it in the slightest. Freedom never meant much until I had it. And while the last few years have been hard, everything now is so good.

"Finish." Casey licks her fingers.

"Good girl. Can you go and wash your hands now?"

"My tongue washed my hands."

I chuckle. Her act makes me laugh every time, and it shouldn't because it's old and not really that funny. She's just lucky she's cute. "I'm sure it did a good job, but I think soap does a better one. Go on."

She runs up the hallway and I shake my head. I love my girl with all my heart. Life's been hard, but she's been a blessing in the darker times. There's no way I'd do anything differently when it comes to Casey.

Gathering up her plate to wash, I take in a deep breath and smile at the thought of Alex coming over. Tonight I'm going to tell him what I couldn't this morning. I'm falling in love with him. And I want to be with him—I just don't know how.

And now Casey's busted us, there's no point in hiding that he's spending nights with me.

After loading the dishwasher, I walk into the living room to find Casey leaning on the coffee table, back to watching TV.

"It's time for bed now, Casey."

"I want this." She points at the screen.

I scoop her up into my arms and nuzzle her neck. She shrieks with laughter. "No. It's bedtime. Let's get teeth brushed and into pyjamas. I'll read you a story."

Her eyes are wide. "*Hairy Maclary*?"

"If you like."

By the time we get to the end of the tale about Hairy Maclary meeting his friends, her little lips are pursed and she snorts before rolling onto her side.

God, how I love this kid with every fibre of my being. She's my everything.

I lean over and brush my lips against her forehead.

She lets out a sigh, raises her hand to rub her nose and her head does that final flop against the pillow that tells me she's deep asleep. I'm sure it's just a phase, but when I read to her, it doesn't take long.

She's so beautiful that I grab my sketch pad from the living room and return to her bedside. It takes me a few moments to capture that look—I can flesh it out later. Maybe when it's more difficult to get her to sleep, I can look back and remember when times were good.

After rising, I walk back through to the living room. Thank god it's Friday. At least if Casey wakes early tomorrow, we don't have to go anywhere.

The tap on the door knocks me out of my thoughts, and I walk, then run.

This is it—I'm going to tell this man how I feel and take a leap.

I jerk the door open.

Alex's blue eyes drink me in. "Are you okay? You look flushed."

"I love you."

His eyebrows rise. "Hello to you too."

"I didn't say it this morning because you surprised me, but I love you too. I want more, but I don't know where to start."

He grins, elation in his eyes, and leans over to kiss me. "I love you too."

Alex lifts his hand. Plastic containers weigh down a bag. "How about we eat first and then we talk about it? I went to the Indian place down the road and got a few different things. I wasn't sure what you liked."

"I'm starved. I'll eat it all if you're not careful."

He laughs, and I step back to let him in.

"How was your day?" I ask.

"Long." He kisses me again. "And I missed you. You're getting to be a habit, Ms Maitland."

My lips twitch, and I bite my bottom lip to control it. "I've been thinking the same thing about you."

His eyes search mine. "What are we going to do about it, Lana? I can't stay forever, and I don't want to leave you behind."

I blink rapidly and nod toward the food. "Let's eat before it gets cold and think about it afterward."

Or maybe we won't.

Because I don't want to think about it. Any of it. I like the way things are right now, and I know it won't last forever, but what other options do I have? We're from two different countries—two different worlds.

We came together under the weirdest circumstances, and who knows how long this will last? It's not like I have a record of long relationships, and I'm not even sure about Alex's background.

I don't really know him that well yet.

But I do know that he makes me feel more special than anyone ever has. Gareth seduced me, but Alex is genuine. He likes me for me.

We laugh about stupid stuff, and I'm not afraid to be myself around him. And Casey adores him. He's everything I ever wanted in a partner.

But can he really be mine?

11

LANA

The next few weeks aren't always easy.

Alex works all kinds of weird hours, and he always make some time for us. It must be tiring for him, but I just make sure when he's not at work, he's getting plenty of rest.

For now, we're finding our way through scheduling obstacles, but I'm mindful of the fact that with each passing week, his leaving grows closer.

Then what will I do?

I'm not sure what would happen if he asked me to leave with him. We're secure here, even if I don't particularly enjoy working for Gareth. It's safe.

And I've always played things safe for Casey.

It'd be a whole different story if it was just me, but it's not. She has to come first.

Always.

Anna stares at me as I cross the room and place my bag on my desk. I pick up my coffee mug. Her eyes bore holes in me until I look up to meet her intense gaze.

I frown. "Is everything okay, Anna?"

My stomach flips as her brows knit. Tension creeps into my shoulders—the silence is unnerving.

"What is it? Has something happened?"

She nods slowly.

"For God's sake, Anna. Just tell me what it is. It can't be *that* bad." *Can it?*

"You're on TMZ," she says.

Huh? "What's that?"

Anna wrinkles her nose. "You don't know what TMZ is and you're dating Alex Stone? It's a celebrity news site."

My heart sinks. "What?"

"Come and have a look."

It's a photo from an afternoon last week. I picked up Casey from day care and we started to walk home only to find Alex waiting for us in the park with a big smile on his face as he'd finished for the day.

There's me on one side, Alex on the other, and my chest squeezes at the sight of Casey in the middle. She's staring up at Alex, awe written all over her face.

"What's this site?"

"I can't believe you don't know." Anna crosses her arms. "It's just one of the biggest entertainment sites in the world."

My throat tightens. "Really?"

"Are you okay, Lana? You've gone really pale."

I stagger back, grab hold of my office chair and sit down. "How big are we talking?"

She shrugs. "Millions of viewers. I'm not sure how big it is here, but it's huge in the States. It says he's having a big romance while he's here, and they're speculating about how your daughter is related to him. Probably because the same thing happened to Josh Carter and that turned out to be his daughter."

Anna keeps talking, but I switch off. Nausea sweeps me. I didn't want attention, and I told Alex that. I thought he knew what he was talking about when he said we'd avoid it here and that his career wasn't big enough to attract it.

And yet here we all are on a website. I don't even know what the story attached to it says yet. I guess technically it's correct—as far as I'm concerned, Alex and I have been falling in love. But the last thing I want is Casey plastered all over the Internet.

I bury my face in my hands.

Click.

I know that sound.

Gareth's office door squeaks as he pulls it open, and he's the last person I feel like facing today. *I wonder if it's too late to pull a sicky.*

"Lana. Could you please join me in my office? I want to give you the criteria for some reports I need."

The door closes with a click.

Sure. Whatever.

Slowly, I rise from my seat. If he wants to talk to me about the website Anna's just shown me, at least I'm prepared for it. Though, given that I haven't really processed it yet, I'm not sure what my response will be.

Anna screws up her face. "Good luck. I know how much work you do on those reports. As if you need more."

I force a smile. "I guess he just wants to make sure he's up to date with the markets. It's kind of his job."

Turning, I sigh and I approach his door. I love the days when he just leaves me alone to do my job and the majority of short conversations we have are work-related. But I've just got a feeling.

As I enter the room, he looks up from his desk as if he's been there working the whole time.

"Close the door and come in."

I suppress an eye roll but do as he asks, then plonk myself down on the chair opposite him.

"Have you got something to tell me?" he asks.

I shrug. "Nothing that's any of your business."

He turns his laptop around. Sure enough, there's the link on display that Anna showed me a few moments ago. "This is my business."

A prickle runs up my neck.

"It's really not. You made that decision a long time ago."

"Melanie sent this to me. She's at home resting after her first IVF treatment and she was excited to see you were happy. And then she cried because she's a big ball of hormones and you have a beautiful little girl."

Crossing my arms, I lean back in the chair. "I'm sorry to hear that, and I hope IVF works for you two. But you opted not to be a part of Casey's life, and this has nothing to do with you.

His nostrils flare. But he's got no leg to stand on. It'd be better for him if Casey and I left, but we've never had anywhere else to go, and he knows it.

"I don't need this. Not right now," he says.

"Neither do I. This is the last thing I wanted. But it's for me to sort out."

"Make sure you do," he snaps.

Frowning, I rise, circling to stand behind my chair and lean on it. Things have been pretty amicable between us so far, and he owes me—not the other way around. But if he wants to get aggressive, I need to stand up to him now—not later.

"Gareth, you made the decision not to be in Casey's life. And I've been fine with that because your wife doesn't deserve what you did, and neither did I. According to that site, there's speculation Casey is Alex's, and if anything, that benefits you. Maybe you should be grateful it's happened."

He splutters. "Are you serious about this guy?"

"I am. Not that it's any of your business either. And Casey loves him. So, I'm not going to stop seeing him."

Besides, I love him too.

Gareth's Adam's apple bobs as he swallows hard. "Just be careful."

"I am. I'm not about to set myself up like I did last time."

He blinks a few times and then drops his gaze, shifting it to the folder in front of him on his desk. "Good. That's all."

With that, I've been dismissed, so I leave his office, returning to my desk.

"Are you okay?" Anna asks.

"Why?"

"You look pissed off."

I shake my head. "There are some things that Gareth just has to sort out himself. I've got work to do."

"Are you going to do anything about these photos?" she asks.

I don't really know how to respond. This isn't a situation I was ready for, but I feel like I should have been prepared for it. I've been swept away by a loving, gentle man who's perfect for me, and all other thoughts have been pushed aside when they really should have been my priority.

"I'm sure Alex will know what to do," she says. "In the meantime, can I make you a coffee?"

I pinch the bridge of my nose. "I'd really appreciate it."

Anna gets up and walks to my desk, plucking my mug from in front of my monitor. "If there's ever anything I can do to help, just ask. And I'm not just saying that because your boyfriend is Alex Stone. I haven't told anyone."

"Thanks, Anna."

I rub my face with my hands and then grab my mouse, giving it a jiggle until the screen wakes up.

This is not going to be an easy day.

WHEN IT'S time to leave, I step out of the office and into the fresh air.

Taking a deep breath, I pause a moment before I set off toward day care. I can't wait to get home with Casey. Home feels like the one safe place right now.

There's a lot of chatter when I get to day care, and I sign the attendance book to say I'm taking Casey home and make my way through to the toddler room.

"Mummy." Casey launches herself at me, and I squat, opening my arms to receive her. I bury my nose in her neck and hold her tight. She wriggles out of my grasp, her blue eyes wide. "There was a lady in the park looking at me."

I frown. "What do you mean?"

Maria walks up behind her. "She's right. The kids were out playing and someone in the park was watching Casey. I brought her inside as it seemed weird. One of the other teachers went out to see if she was okay, but the woman ran off."

I bite my bottom lip. Maria's brows knit. "Are you okay?"

"Not really. It's been a really screwy day and it's not over yet. Thank you for taking care of Casey."

Casey hugs Maria's leg.

"That's what I do. If there's anything else you need, let me know."

I straighten up. "I'm not sure yet, but I will."

"We'll be on the lookout tomorrow just in case. Hopefully it was a one-off." Her smile is reassuring, but I'm not so sure there's nothing to worry about. This has to be related to that stupid website. Surely.

I don't even know who to be angry with.

Alex should know better but clearly didn't. I have been naive, apparently.

And I can't let Casey see any of that. She needs to think everything is fine and normal.

"Let's go home, Casey." I hold out my hand and give her a hug when she takes it.

She beams. "Home time?"

I laugh. "Yes, it's home time, sweet girl."

Walking this way isn't fun. This is the park we were photographed in, and none of us had any idea.

I'll use the car every day from tomorrow.

I switch on the TV as soon as we walk in the door and change the channel to cartoons. I'm too agitated to worry about Casey spending too much time in front of it.

Alex will still be on set so I can't call him for advice.

I get up and close the curtains. It's still early, but the unease that someone is watching us is overwhelming.

My first instinct is to hide from the world with Casey. But that's not a practical solution.

I love Alex. He's turned my world upside down with his love and kindness. And he's taken on a role in Casey's life without hesitation.

I'm not sure what lies in the future, but I do want to be with him.

This is too big for either of us to ignore.

Me: *Call me when you get this.*

Casey chews away on her muesli bar, her eyes glued to the television. Thoughts churn in my head. I was aware our relationship might have a publicity issue, but Alex and I settled into things being so normal. I forgot about my concerns.

I close my eyes to try and steady my nerves.

Relief pours through me as the ringing sound of my phone comes from the coffee table, and I pick it up and sigh.

"Alex?" My voice wobbles, but I can't help it.

"Hey, you okay?" he asks. His concerned tone nearly brings tears to my eyes.

"Did you know someone took photos of us?" My voice comes out in a croaky whisper.

"What? What's happened? I'm on my way."

I'm left staring at the phone as he disconnects.

"Mummy, I'm hungry." Casey leaps at me, squishing herself against my side.

I lean over and kiss her forehead. "I'll get dinner started. Alex is on his way."

"Daddy will take care of that lady."

My eyebrows rise. Despite our best efforts, she's determined not to let that go. Whatever happens between Alex and I in the future, I think he'll always be 'Daddy' to her.

"He's a good man," I say.

"I love him."

I smile down at her. With her blue eyes, she could pass as Alex's daughter. My concern is that these photos are going to cause awkward questions. "I know you do."

She climbs up onto the couch and wraps her arms around my neck. "I love you, Mummy."

I turn my head and place a kiss on her temple. "I love you too, Casey. More than the moon."

"More than *Hairy Maclary*?"

I laugh. She loves that book so much. "Even more than him."

I'm still cuddled up with her on the couch when there's a tap on the door.

"Lana? It's me."

"It's Daddy." Casey springs off the couch and runs toward the sound. I rise from the couch and walk to her, unlocking and opening the door to Alex's concerned expression.

"Are you okay?" he asks.

I take a step back and let him in, shutting and locking the door behind him. "We're on some website. TMZ?"

He pales. "Shit. Really?"

"Yes, really. The same thing I was worried about, but you told me it'd be fine." I fist my hand; I'm so frustrated. "And then something happened at day care."

"What happened?"

"Daddy, Daddy. There was a lady at day care looking at me today." Casey tugs at his jeans, and he frowns before shifting his gaze to me.

"Maria said there was someone in the park taking an interest in Casey. It made her uncomfortable." I walk away and flop onto the couch. "I think they're related."

He scoops up Casey and carries her into the room where he joins me on the couch with her on his lap.

"It wouldn't surprise me."

"You said—"

He pops a kiss on Casey's head and lowers her to the ground, then gathers me into his arms. "I didn't think that kind of thing would happen. I'm in a small town in New Zealand, not central LA."

"Well, apparently they have cameras here too."

He presses his nose into my hair. "I'll call my manager. I had a couple of missed calls from him while I was filming. It was you I called back first."

"Should think so." I sniff. "Priorities."

"You got it."

I turn my head, and he presses his forehead to mine. "We'll sort this out. I promise."

"You'd better."

He pulls away, and concern lingers in his eyes. They're filled with an emotion I understand, and I love him all the more for it. But I can't change this. This is on him.

"I'll get onto it in the morning. Right now, I want to just hold you because you look like you need it," he murmurs.

"Is that your way of saying I look like shit?"

He chuckles and kisses my temple. "No, you look beautiful as always. I think we need to not go out in public together for a little while. Until I work out what to do."

I nod. "I figured as much."

"I'm sorry, Lana." He takes a deep breath in my hair. "I should have known better, but I didn't. The casting announcement isn't out yet, but it can't be far away. I know that will be news."

"It could get worse?"

He pulls back, looking into my eyes. I don't need him to answer from the way he's frowning.

"I—"

"Well, that's all we need. I should have thought more about this."

Alex strokes my back. "How about I order pizza delivery and we talk this through?" He tilts his head. "We'll work it out. I know we will."

"We have to, because this is the one thing I was scared of."

"I know."

"Daddy, did you say pizza?" Casey pats him on the arm.

Despite myself, I laugh. "Yes, sweetheart. Alex said he'd order pizza."

She holds her arms in the air. "Yay!"

AFTER PIZZA and some time together, Casey falls asleep while I read to her.

I lean over and place a kiss on her temple.

She's what's important here—I can't lose focus on that even if my heart wants me to.

I let out a sigh and walk into the living room, running my fingers through my hair.

Alex looks up. I open my mouth to say something just as he speaks up.

He's on the phone.

I sit beside him and he takes my hand in his, squeezing it tight.

"Okay. I'll talk to Lana and let you know. Thanks for that."

He disconnects the call and drops his phone on the coffee table. "That was Charlie. My agent. I thought I'd call him back tonight instead of waiting until tomorrow."

"What did he say?"

He draws in a deep breath. "Well, the news of my casting is about to drop. He can ask for it to be delayed, but it might already be too late."

I nod. "Okay."

"And he's sorry about what's happened. We can get security if you want it."

"Security?"

"For you and Casey."

I blink rapidly, trying to process what he's just said. "That's a bit over the top, isn't it?"

"Just to make sure you're safe."

"I ... I don't know."

He places a kiss on my hand. "You don't have to make up your mind right now. I think you should use the car instead of walking in the meantime. And we'll stay in instead of going anywhere."

I swallow hard. "That works for me."

"We can get through this, babe. This is all new to me too. I've had media stories written about me, but nothing like this before."

I close my eyes, and he pulls me into his arms. "Why don't we go to bed and get some sleep before tomorrow. I just want to hold you."

Nodding, I bury my face in his neck. I just don't want to think anymore tonight.

I'M STILL numb in the morning, dropping Casey off at day care. Using the car surely makes it less likely anyone will take photos of us. *Won't it?*

The problem is that I don't know, and Alex can't give me any kind of definitive answer. It leaves me conflicted and confused.

I want him. I don't want all these things that come with him.

But I can't choose one or the other. It's all or nothing.

And the thought of that breaks my heart.

The morning drags as I'm distracted at every turn. I look up every time I spot movement in the large window out the front of my office from the corner of my eye.

Anna makes me coffee and then keeps to herself as she seems to sense I'm not really myself today.

I just don't know what to do. Maybe I should have taken the day off.

Even Gareth looks at me sideways as I drop his latest report on his desk, but says nothing.

My mood seems obvious to everyone, and that's the last thing I care about.

I'm a few minutes from walking out the door at the end of the day when my mobile rings. My heart sinks at the sight of 'day care' on the screen.

"Hello?"

"Lana, it's Maria. I don't want you to panic, but we need you to come now."

I swallow hard. "What's happened?"

"A woman just tried to grab Casey."

12

———

LANA

My heart stops.

"What?" I whisper.

"She's safe. But the police are on their way. Try to keep calm," she says.

"Keep calm?" I screech. I don't mean to. Casey is safe, but it's impossible not to freak out.

Gareth's office door flies open. "What's going on?"

"Lana." Maria keeps her even tone, but that's probably for my benefit because I know how much she loves my daughter. "I have her right here. They're already pulling CCTV footage in the office. Take your time and get here safely."

"Lana? Are you okay?" Anna stands over my desk, and I look up at her and blink.

"Lana," Gareth says.

"Lana." Maria's in my ear again, and I have to focus on her.

"Sorry, Maria. I'll be there as soon as I can. Please look after Casey."

"I've got her."

I disconnect the call. Gareth grips my shoulder. "What's wrong?"

"Someone ... someone tried to grab Casey from day care."

"What?" Anna gasps.

"Grab your things. I'll take you," Gareth says.

I blink rapidly, trying to hold back tears. "You don't—"

"I'm not giving you a choice. You're not in any state to drive. Or probably even walk."

Anna rubs my arm. "Gareth's right. You should let him drive you."

I close my eyes for a moment and steady my breathing. My car's parked just down the road, but my hands are shaking too much to drive it. "Thank you."

I swore the world would have to be ending before I accepted anything more from Gareth Turner. But right now, I just need to hold my baby.

"I'll have to get her car seat out of my car."

He nods. "Whatever you need to do. Anna, can you please call Melanie and let her know what's happened? I'll be late home."

"Sure." Her brows knit in concern, but I force a small smile.

"Thank you. Both of you. I just need to be with her."

"Of course. Come on," Gareth says.

I lead Gareth to my car where I take out Casey's seat. He stands, fiddling with his tie as I set it up in the back seat of his car. While I appreciate him driving me, by the time I've done that, I'm not shaking quite as much. But my heart's still pounding fast.

He's already in the driver's seat when I climb in the other side.

"Where are we going?" he asks.

It's stupid. I know I shouldn't be disappointed, but of course Gareth doesn't know where Casey goes to day care. He pays for half of it, but he puts that money into my salary and I make all the arrangements.

I give him the address, and he nods. "I know where that is. We'll be there really soon."

Pulling my phone out of my bag, I dial Alex.

Please answer. Please answer. Please ...

"Hey, beautiful."

"Alex." I breathe in, but it comes out sounding like a hiccough.

"Is everything okay?" Alex's gentle tones calm me a little, but I clutch my phone to my ear, sucking in short breaths while the world still threatens to turn black.

"No." I let out a sob.

"What's going on?"

"Someone just tried to snatch Casey from day care."

"What the fuck? Where are you?"

"Gareth is taking me to there. The police are on their way. I just want to get there and hold her."

"Okay. Um. Give me a little time, and I'll see if I can get out of here."

"Thank you." I wipe a stray tear off my cheek. "I know you're busy working."

"I love you. I'll be there as soon as I can."

"Love you too," I whisper.

I drop my phone back in my bag and scrub my face with my palms.

"That serious, huh?" Gareth asks.

I narrow my gaze as I turn my head to look at him. "Are you kidding right now?"

"Sorry."

Thankfully, he shuts up the rest of the way, and as soon as he comes to a stop outside day care, I open the door and run.

The office is just inside the front door, and several of the teachers are gathered right by it.

"Mummy!" Casey pushes her way through the group and

throws herself into my arms, and I grip her tight, closing my eyes. This is *my* baby. Tears prick my eyes.

"Hey." I kiss her hair over and over. *Mine.*

"That lady was here."

"I know."

Maria places her hand on my arm. "The good news is that we got some really clear shots on the security camera."

I blow out a breath. "Good. Are the police here yet?"

The door behind me opens, and in walks Gareth, flanked by two police officers. They head into the office while Gareth joins me.

"This is ..." I swallow and take a moment to refocus. "This is my boss. He was concerned so he drove me here rather than me driving myself."

Maria nods. "Understandable. You must be shaken up."

"You Mummy's boss?" Casey stares at Gareth, wide-eyed.

His lips are drawn into a tight smile. "I am. I'll wait and give you a lift home when you're ready, Lana."

"Thank you." I give Casey a squeeze and she squeals.

"No, Mummy. Don't hug me too tight."

"I'm sorry. I'm just so glad you're okay." I cover her face with kisses. I shift my gaze to Maria. "What happened?"

"The kids were on their way back in for morning tea, and Casey wanted to bring the toy she'd been playing with inside, so she popped back out. I looked out the window to make sure she was okay, and the woman must have said something to her, as then Casey ran to the gate."

I suck in a painful breath. Is this what's come out of the way Alex and I met? Does Casey now think it's okay just to go over to strangers? A million thoughts race through my head, and I hold my baby tight again.

"Ouch, Mummy," Casey whines.

"I'm sorry, sweetheart. Mummy's just a little scared."

"If I hadn't looked out the window when I did ..." Maria's eyes are full of fear.

"You always take good care of her. I know you do. Please don't think I'm angry at you."

"Anyway, the woman opened the gate just as I rounded the corner of the building and she was squatting with her arms open like she was waiting for Casey to give her a hug. As soon as she saw me, she stood and ran away."

"Casey, you can't go to strangers like that." I place a kiss in her hair.

"She said she knew Daddy. He wants to see me." She slots her index finger in her mouth the way she does when she's thinking about something.

Behind me, Gareth clears his throat.

"Honey, if Alex wants to see you, he'll be here with me. He won't send a friend. Do you understand?"

She screws up her face. This is a lot for her to take in. She's so warm and friendly, and I hate to seed mistrust in her, but she has to learn that not everyone is going to be as good as Alex.

"Okay. Only Daddy."

I nod. "That's right." I eye Gareth. "Only Daddy."

The police are wonderful. A female constable talks to Casey while she sits on my lap, and Casey makes me smile at the way she goes into graphic detail about everything.

"And then the lady said she was Daddy's friend, and Daddy wants to see me."

The police woman looks at me. "And this was no one you knew?"

I shake my head. "No."

"Is her father here?"

I resist the urge to glance at Gareth. "Casey calls my boyfriend Daddy. He's at work right now."

"Daddy's in a movie." Casey clasps her hands together.

"My boyfriend is Alex Stone. He's an actor, and he's on set filming today." I blow out a breath. "I don't know for sure, but I do wonder if this is something to do with him."

She frowns. "What do you mean?"

"There were photos of us on a website yesterday. TMZ?"

Her eyebrows rise.

"Anyway, I've been concerned about someone being out there watching us to take more, and then Casey said a woman was watching her yesterday, and now this today."

The constable writes it all in her notebook and nods. "We'll be in touch when we have any information."

"Is it likely you'll get her?" Gareth asks.

"We'll do our best."

It takes everything in me not to tell him to bugger off, but he's taking us home and he's got my car seat.

Maria swoops in and gives Casey a kiss on the top of her head. She straightens up and rubs my arm. "I know it's hard, but try not to stress. See you tomorrow?"

"We'll see." I force a smile.

"I understand. Just let us know."

"Thank you."

For a moment when I step outside, I'm disorientated. My instinct is to look for my own car, but of course it's not there, and I blow out a breath as Gareth walks past me.

When we get to his vehicle, I strap Casey into her car seat and get into the front seat.

"This not our car, Mummy," she says.

I glance at Gareth. "No, sweetheart. Gareth is driving us home. Mummy was a bit shaken up about what happened."

"Where's Daddy?"

Raising my right hand, I rub the side of my cheek so I don't have to see the look on Gareth's face. "Alex will see us at home. He's trying to get out of work early."

"She already calls him Daddy?" he asks.

I cross my arms and shrug. "It's not that Alex and I asked her to." Meeting his gaze, all I see is a confused man—and yet one who has not take responsibility for his daughter. "She's never had anyone like that in her life, Gareth. Casey chose this."

He starts the car and our short drive is in silence until he pulls up to the kerb.

"I'll stay with you until Alex arrives." He unbuckles his seatbelt.

"You don't have to do that."

He looks in the rear view mirror at Casey who beams back at him. "I don't know if I'll feel right otherwise."

After I remove her car seat, we go inside and Gareth sits in a living room chair.

I fist my hands. The last thing I want is to start anything in front of Casey.

"Where's Daddy?" Casey asks.

"I told you, sweetheart. He's at work. But he'll be here soon. You just have to be patient."

She looks at Gareth. "You Garef?"

He clamps his lips together, I presume to stop laughing, and nods. "I'm Gareth."

"You Mummy's friend?"

His eyes meet mine, and I just feel numb. He devastated me, but there's nothing between us now. Just some regret that he never wanted anything to do with Casey.

"I am." He smiles, and there's a sadness about him that radiates through the room. What he and Melanie are going through has to be tough.

"My daddy is coming home soon."

He looks up at me again, but I refuse to meet his gaze. "You sound like you're very excited about that."

"I am. Want to watch *Paw Patrol*?" Casey asks.

I hold up my palms. "How about I make some coffee? I'll make you a hot chocolate, Casey. And we can all watch *Paw Patrol* until Alex gets here." Shifting my gaze to Gareth, I draw in a breath. "Shouldn't you call Melanie and let her know you're here?"

He shrugs. "I sent her a text."

"Doesn't she think it's weird that you're at my place?"

He tilts his head. "She understands that I'm helping out a friend." Drawing in a loud breath, he looks around the room, and it makes me grind my teeth. "Besides, she'd never forgive me if anything happened and I could have been here to help."

By the time I make coffee and hot chocolate, and we've watched an episode of *Paw Patrol*, I'm just about climbing the walls.

Not only because Alex isn't here yet, but because that woman is still out there. How can I take Casey outside ever again? How can I trust the people around us?

There's a tap on the door. Gareth rises.

I roll my eyes. "Sit down."

By some miracle, he obeys.

"Lana, it's me."

Just the sound of Alex's voice brings tears to my eyes, and I fling open the door and throw my arms around his neck.

"Hey. It's okay." He buries his nose under my ear and just holds me.

This is what I needed. My fear might have hold of me right

now, but Alex soothes that just by being present. He walks me backward into the room and closes the door behind him.

Casey rushes across the room, wrapping herself around Alex's leg.

I look across at Gareth. "Alex is here now. You can go."

Gareth grunts, but he stands. He opens his mouth to say something, but a knock on the door stops him in his tracks.

Who on earth could that be?

Alex is still right behind me as I open the door.

"Lana Maitland?" a tall woman with short, dark hair addresses me.

"Yes?"

"Detective Carsons. Can I come in?"

"Please." I step back. Gareth sits back down on one of the recliners. "Um, this is my boyfriend, Alex. And that's my boss, Gareth Turner."

She nods toward both of them. Alex nods in return.

"Please take a seat." I nod toward the empty recliner, and she sits while Alex and I sit on the couch. "Casey, honey. How about you go and play in your room for a little while?"

"I want to watch Paw Patrol."

I stroke her cheek. "I know, but I just need to talk with this lady. I'll get you an ice cream if you do this for me."

Her eyes widen. "But dinner ..."

"Just this once I'll let you have one before dinner."

I don't need to ask her twice. She zooms off to her room without even looking behind her. Beside me, Alex chuckles.

Shifting my gaze to Detective Carsons, I swallow hard. "Do you have an update?"

"The good news is that we've found the woman responsible for today's incident."

Relief floods my system. The last thing I needed was someone still running around out there who tried to grab my child. "Who is she? What did she want?"

Detective Carsons pauses for a moment. "You told the constable you were concerned about the photos on the TMZ website, didn't you?"

I nod. My stomach sinks.

"This was related to the photos," the detective says. "One of Mr Stone's fans tried to abduct your daughter."

13

ALEX

This is a nightmare.

I've never felt so helpless.

"She's part of an online group who have been debating whether Mr Stone is Casey's father," the detective explains.

"Wait. What?" I ask.

Lana's neck just about swivels 180 as she looks back at me. "It's those damn photos, Alex."

"The perpetrator is fifteen."

I stare at the officer. "What?"

"Her parents are distraught and very apologetic. They had no idea."

Lana blows out a long breath. "Fifteen."

"She says that she only wanted to ask Casey who her father was. And she knows she took it way too far."

"So, what happens now?" Lana croaks. It was screwed up enough that someone attempted this—even more so that it's a kid.

"That's up to you. Her parents are making her write an apology letter to you. We can charge her, but—"

"I don't want that. But I do want the fear of God put into her so she doesn't do anything so stupid again," Lana says.

"Don't you think—" Gareth speaks.

Lana holds up her hand. "She's a kid. And I will do my best to stop Casey doing anything stupid in her life, but she just might do something dumb in the future too."

"Are you sure?" I ask her.

She turns her head to look at me. "She'll be punished by her parents. Lord knows I did some reckless shit when I was a teenager."

I reach for one of her hands and squeeze it. "Whatever you want. I'll support you."

Gareth snorts.

Detective Carsons looks between us as if she's missed something.

"Thank you, Detective," Lana says.

She hands Lana a card and a slip of paper. "I'll co-ordinate delivering this apology, but call me in the meantime if you need anything. There's your case number, too, with the details on how to contact victim support."

"Thank you."

Looking between Gareth and I, she fixes her gaze on me. "I don't know what's happening between you two, but Casey and Lana need your support right now."

I nod. "Agreed."

Gareth just grunts.

"Goodnight." She steps out of the door.

Lana closes it, turning back toward us. "Fifteen. I just—"

"This wouldn't have happened if you were more responsible with who you dated."

I gape at Gareth while Lana sets her jaw.

"I beg your pardon?"

"This is *your* fault, Lana. I—"

"Enough." Lana yells, holding up her palms on either side of her head. "Go home to your wife, Gareth." Lana knits her fingers together and sits on the couch beside me.

Gareth's eyes meet mine. His stony expression tells me he's not too happy about it, but he stands. "I'll leave you to it." He shifts his gaze to Lana. "Don't worry about coming into work tomorrow. Take a few days off. I'll make sure you're paid for them."

"Thank you."

He glares at me. "You'd better have a plan on how to unfuck all this."

"Just go." Lana doesn't even look at him. "This has nothing to do with you."

He scowls and storms out, slamming the front door behind him.

I wrap my arm around her. "I'm so, so sorry."

Lana buries her face in her hands. "This is all such a mess."

"It's my fault. I should have realised that eventually something like this might happen."

She looks up. Her eyes are so tired, and I hate that I'm responsible for this. And there's no shying away from that fact. This wouldn't have happened if it wasn't for me.

"I think you should go too," she says.

I swallow hard. "Are you sure?"

"I'm going to spend the evening with Casey and crawl into bed with her for the night. I just want her near me."

"Lana, I—"

"I know you love me. I love you too. Today was just really hard."

"Come here." I fold my arms around her and bury my face in her hair. "Call me tomorrow. I just want to know you're okay."

"I will," she whispers.

I kiss the top of her head then, reluctantly, I stand. She keeps her gaze down, and it's frustrating. I get that she's scared, but I want to be the one to remove that fear. Even if I am responsible for it.

Driving away is the hardest thing I've ever had to do.

I love her.

I want us to be a family.

IT'S NOT until seven the next evening that my phone buzzes.

Lana: *Can you come over?*

My stomach sinks to my feet. It might be nothing, but I don't have a good feeling about this.

There's a part of me that wants to put this off, but I can't. I have to convince Lana that we can face this together and emerge stronger. I'll do whatever I can to protect her and Casey.

My heart aches that I wasn't able to protect them from what's already happened.

The difficult part is convincing her to look forward and not back.

She drops her gaze as soon as she opens the door. I move to wrap my arms around her, but she steps back to let me in instead.

Shit.

"Are you okay?"

She shrugs, turning away from the door. I follow her into the living room.

"Where's Casey?" I ask.

"She had dinner early and crashed." Her voice is so monotone —her mood obvious. She's not happy, and she has every right to feel that way. I'm the one who assured her we'd be fine.

Lana sits on the couch, and I take a seat beside her.

"Gareth called and asked me if I was taking Casey to the US. You know, it's the first time he's shown any interest in her. He's pretended she doesn't exist since I was pregnant with her."

I take her hand in mine, rubbing my thumb over her knuckle. "What did you say to him?"

She meets my gaze, her blue eyes shimmering with tears. "Told him it was none of his business." Raising her hand to her cheek, she wipes away stray drops. "He's just worried that Melanie will find out if people go digging into my past.

Wrapping my arm around her shoulders, I pull her in tight against me. "I'm so sorry. This is the last thing I thought would happen. It's just so laid-back and nice here, I never thought for a moment that there'd be the interest in me—in us."

Lana lets out a big sigh. "I guess we got that wrong."

"I did. It's my fault. You raised it as a concern, and *I* got it wrong." I kiss the top of her head. "I was thinking all day. I'm going to call Reece and ask him for advice. He's probably the most famous person I know."

She's quiet for a moment—way too quiet. Her fingernails rake her thigh,

"I've been thinking too. I don't think we should see each other anymore."

What?" I release her. "No."

She blinks back tears. "We have secrets in our lives that have to stay buried. I can't risk Casey being exposed to this. What if next time someone does manage to snatch her? What then?"

I'm not sure how to react. She's right. I put them both at risk just by being in their lives, but then, I should be the one to protect them.

And I don't know how.

"I can't go through this again." She buries her head in her hands. "Casey is what's important."

I reach out and stroke her hair. "I don't have to rush back to the States. I'll stay while we work through this."

She meets my gaze. It rips me up inside to see the despair in her eyes. "That's not enough. I need to protect my family now. You need to leave."

I swallow hard. She's putting up barriers all over again, and she's already so far behind them, there's no way I can reach her.

"Lana, we can work through this. Please."

Her eyes fill with more tears. "I don't want to do this, but we both knew this wouldn't last."

My heart rips in two. "What do you mean?"

"You'll finish your film and leave. You've got a whole new world waiting out there for you, Alex. One I won't be a part of."

I shake my head. "You're my world. I want to take you with me. You and Casey. We could start a new life together as a family."

She sniffs, cupping my cheek with her palm. "I can't live like this. One story and someone tries to grab my child? And you're asking me to leave the security I have here to move across the world to an uncertain future."

"I'm certain about us. Aren't you?"

"You're the best thing that's ever happened to me."

Yes. I feel the same, completely the same.

Her lips twitch. "And the worst."

The words cut deep, but I know what she means. She's scared.

And I'll leave for tonight, but I'm not giving up on us.

This isn't over.

14

ALEX

I can't think straight.

For the next two days, I screw up and I screw up big time. I'd gained a reputation for doing solo scenes in one take. Not right now. I flub my lines, I miss my marks, and the last thing I want to do is work.

I came to New Zealand to work, not fall in love.

And now I'm failing at both.

Everyone around me is sympathetic. Word has spread about the TMZ story, and I have the support of all the cast and crew.

It's probably just as well that once I've got through these scenes, they're my last of the movie.

And then the casting announcement hits.

It should be the happiest day of my life.

But my heart's just not in it knowing I can't be with the one person I want to share this moment with.

It doesn't matter how many people congratulate me. It doesn't matter that this is the biggest career step I've taken.

I'm miserable without Lana and Casey.

All I can do is hope that they're okay.

On the third morning, I call Reece. Surely, he must have handled intrusions into his personal life, and there's something about him that makes me think I can trust him. We don't know each other well, but he's someone I've looked up to these past few years, and I hope we come out of the movie we're making together as friends.

I lie on the couch in my living room and take a deep breath.

"Alex?" he asks as he answers the call. A loud thud comes from behind him.

"Hey, Reece. I wondered if you had a minute?"

"Sure thing," he drawls. "Sorry about the noise. We're moving equipment into Pania's workshop. She's starting a fashion business and we've given her some office space. Today is setup day." He pauses. "I saw the announcement go out."

I swallow hard. "Yeah. Thanks."

"You don't sound too enthusiastic. I hope you're not having second thoughts?"

I shift my gaze to the ceiling. "I was wondering if you could give me some advice."

"Give me a second." The background noise fades until it's gone. "That's better. How can I help?"

I draw in a deep breath. "I'm not really sure where to start. I don't know if you remember, but when we went to dinner, I told you I met someone."

"Uh-huh."

"Things have gone a bit crazy. Even before the announcement. We ended up on TMZ and some fan tried to grab my girlfriend's daughter from day care."

There's silence for a moment. "Grab her?"

"Yeah. Some fifteen-year-old trying to find out if Casey's my daughter." I run my fingers through my hair. "I didn't ... I didn't think we'd attract that much attention."

He blows out a breath. "That's a tough one. Pania and I

managed to fly under the radar for quite a while. Josh had some issues with the media when he got back together with Delaney, his wife. I'll talk to him if that helps."

"I'd appreciate it. I just don't know what to do." I close my eyes. "My girlfriend broke up with me over it."

"Shit, dude. I'm so sorry."

We chat a while longer, but I'm not much closer to finding a solution.

What the hell do I do now?

15

LANA

After a few days off, I'm restless. But it's the end of the week, and Casey and I start next week with a clean slate.

Not seeing Alex hurts so much, but I had to make the break. Someone thought their need for gossip about his life was more important than my child's safety, and even if this attempt failed, we might not be as lucky next time.

The evenings are the worst part.

Casey's asleep, and I just miss Alex. By this time of night, he's usually here and I'm in his arms while we just talk before going to bed.

Now the living room seems cold and lifeless. I never noticed it before.

I don't even feel like drawing.

My phone rings, and an unknown number comes up on the screen. I'm always in two minds about what to do with these. I'm not listed anywhere, and I only really keep the phone for the internet and if I have to make appointments.

At least if it's a scam call, it'll give me something to do.

"Hello."

"Hi, Lana. It's Delaney Carter here."

Holy cow. Josh Carter's wife? What is she doing, calling me?

"Hi." I squeak.

"I haven't caught you at a bad time, have I?" she asks.

I look around the room. Why, I have no idea. It's not like she can see, and the living room is as tidy as it always is—fairly neat, with a few toys and a basket of washing in the corner.

"No. My little girl, Casey has just gone to sleep and I was just about to watch some TV."

"Are you two okay?"

Her caring tone nearly makes my eyes prick with tears. I don't want to cry again, but just having someone on the other end of the line who's checking up on me without obligation is overwhelming.

"I think we will be."

"Good. I hope you don't mind me calling, but Alex called Reece for some advice, and Reece spoke to us because we've had issues with photos being taken of our kids—our daughter when we lived back home. Thankfully, we haven't had anyone do anything more than that. You must be so scared."

I sniff. "Terrified. If the day care weren't as observant, or if that girl had a more sinister motive ..."

"Doesn't matter what her motives were. It scared the shit out of you. And I know you're not going to be over that any time soon. We were lucky and I had both my bestie and a supportive community ..." She pauses. "Alex seemed to indicate you were, well, on your own."

I break down—the stress of the past few days decides to come out all at once while this stranger is on the phone comforting me. "I'm so sorry for doing this. It's just been such a difficult week."

"It's okay," she says. "I have my girls and I understand. Just know you're not alone."

"Thank you." I reach for a tissue from the box on the coffee table and wipe my face. "I haven't really had anyone to talk to."

"I figured. And I'm here for you if you need someone. I've been in your shoes—not to that extent, but I know what it's like to worry. It's such a fucked up thing to have to deal with."

I blow my nose. "It really is."

She seems to hesitate again before responding. "Alex also told Reece that you two broke up because of what happened. Are you okay?"

I sigh. "Maybe I will be in time. I don't know."

"It's a shame you're all the way over there. It'd be so much easier if you were closer."

Running my hand through my hair, I lie back on the couch. "I wish I was too. I love your cooking videos. They came right as Casey started eating more solids, and she just loves your mac and cheese."

Delaney laughs. "I officially love you now. When I meet people, usually the first thing they say is which of Josh's movies they like. I mean, who cares about his career—what about me?"

I snort and then cover my nose with my hand with embarrassment.

"Oh, I think you'd fit in well here, Lana. But you have to do what's best for you and Casey. Just again know that I'm here if you need me."

"Thank you."

"You're welcome. I was a single mum. When I fell pregnant with my eldest, my mum threw me out, but I had my bestie, Pania, and her family. They took me in. Sounds like you're doing a hell of a job on your own."

I well up again. "I appreciate that. And I had no idea."

"It's not really public knowledge. I'm not ashamed of it, but I know what it's like to be left out in the cold. So, I really do mean it when I say I'm here for anything you need. I was lucky that Josh had been living in this world for a while before I joined him. He knew how to take care of us." She pauses. "I think Alex really loves you, but he's still working out how this life works for him, let alone bringing a family into it."

"How do you handle the fans?"

She snorts. "They can be so invasive. Josh thinks I'm crazy for doing it, but I do monitor some of the more extreme fans for myself. Some of them think our marriage is fake and he's in some secret relationship with Gabby Reynolds."

My eyebrows rise. "No way."

"Some of them even requested copies of our marriage certificate."

"How do you cope with that?"

Delaney chuckles. "Good friends and wine. I cope by keeping an eye on it because I think I'd be more crazy if I couldn't see. All I'm worried about is keeping my kids safe."

I blink back tears. "I was so scared," I whisper.

"I bet you were. I'm so glad you're both okay."

"Thank you."

"And don't think I'm pushing you to get back together with Alex, either. I haven't even met the guy. You have to do what's best for you and your girl. If anyone understands that, it's me."

I swallow hard.

"So, if you need a friend, or just someone to talk to, I'm here. I'll text you all my contact details."

"Thank you."

I sit in the quiet for a while after the call's finished. Part of me still can't believe that Delaney Carter took the time out to call me and talk. She must have a million other things to do with her day. And she's so funny, and down to earth, and ...

If we ever meet, I have to stop fangirling over her.

Alex reassured me that we wouldn't get this kind of attention, but it wasn't him downplaying the situation. It was his inexperience that caused him to promise things he couldn't predict.

And now, the opposite has happened.

Delaney's right. This won't necessarily go away just because I made the break.

So, what the hell do I do?

16

LANA

The universe delivers its answer on Monday.

"Mummy. I don't want day care. Mummy!" Casey screeches from the back seat of the car.

"I'm so sorry, honey. But I have to go back to work today. You haven't seen Maria in a while, won't that be fun?" I let out a sigh and keep driving.

I couldn't face the walk this morning. I'm tired and grumpy from not sleeping over my decision to break up with Alex, and Casey's been the same—probably for the same reason.

She's asked me about 'Daddy' about five hundred times since we last saw Alex. And while I'm still in love with him, I have no idea what to do about our situation. I'm not even sure if the decision I've made is the right one.

I can't go back in time and stop those pictures of us bringing attention to Casey and me. I also don't know if breaking up with Alex will stop any speculation.

Maria swoops in like an angel when we get to day care, and once again, I'm so grateful for her. I'd give anything to keep staying at home with Casey instead of going to work, but I know she's in good hands. If Maria hadn't been so cautious, I hate to think what might have happened. And getting back into our routine is important to try and return to a sense of normalcy.

By mid-morning, my head pounds, and it's like I have a team of carpenters in my brain building a house. And, despite taking painkillers, nothing's making it better.

If anything, it's getting worse.

"Are you okay?" Gareth surprises me with his question as he walks past my desk, coffee mug in hand. The only thing he's ever been concerned about is Melanie not finding out about Casey. It's probably the first time he's ever enquired about my health.

"I've got a headache. I'm sure I'll be fine."

"Go home if you're not feeling well."

I raise an eyebrow at him. "I've only just got back to work after all the drama last week."

"You should go home, Lana. There's no colour in your cheeks," Anna says from behind her desk.

"Maybe." I still hesitate because if I get behind on these reports, it'll be a crash course for Anna to learn them.

"Well, it's your call." Gareth doesn't hang around and heads back into his office.

I let out a long breath and then sigh when my mobile vibrates on my desk. I groan as I see 'day care' appear on the screen.

Picking it up, I press the button to accept. "Hello?"

"Lana, it's Maria. I'm so sorry to be calling you like this, but Casey has chickenpox. We need you to come and collect her."

My head swims. "But how ...?"

"She's not alone. There are three of them going home." Her kind tone makes me want to cry. My stomach pitches at the thought that I dropped Casey off this morning without realising she was sick. "I'm on my way."

After disconnecting the call, I walk into Gareth's office. He's hunched over his desk, and I tap on the open door to get his attention.

"Casey has chickenpox. I'm going to need some time off."

His brow furrows. "Any chance you have it?"

I pause. I never had it as a child. And I have been feeling awful … "I'm not sure."

He covers his nose and mouth with his hand as if I haven't been in the office all morning as he's walked back and forwards. "Then, go. Don't worry about the leave. I'll make sure you're paid."

Usually, I'd give him shit about not caring about his own daughter, but today I just feel crappy and want to go home. "Thanks. Haven't you had chickenpox?"

He nods. "Yes, and so has Melanie, but I don't want to take any bugs home."

Right.

Returning to my desk, I throw my things in my bag and pick it up. "I'll be back when … sometime." I look at Anna and shrug.

"What's wrong?" Anna asks.

"Chickenpox."

Her eyes widen. "Haven't you had it? I heard it's much worse as an adult. I got vaccinated."

Thanks. "I'm not sure about that, but if Casey's got it, it stands to reason I have because I've never had it. I hope it's not too bad."

She nods. "Me too. Call me if you need anything."

I would say the same thing, but the last thing I need is to deal with work crap while I'm sick. "Thank you."

The cool air hits me when I walk out the door, and I take a deep breath. Just being outside is a relief.

It even helps my headache a little.

Maria greets me at the door to day care with Casey.

I scoop her up onto my hip and she wraps her arms around my neck. Her bottom lip wobbles as tears fill her eyes. "I told you, Mummy."

Kissing her cheek, I hug her tight. "I'm sorry." I look up at Maria. "I feel so awful. I should have realised something was off this morning."

Maria shakes her head. "Don't beat yourself up over it. We get this in waves, and the spots show up where you'd least expect. It's not until they become more widespread that people see them sometimes." She's being so kind, and I just want to cry. "Will you be okay at home?"

I nod. "I'll order grocery delivery and we'll hibernate for a bit."

"Sounds like a great plan." She gives me a kind smile. "If you need anything, give me a call."

"Thank you."

I've never been so relieved to see my front door, and I take a deep breath of home as I step inside.

"I'm sick." Casey sounds so forlorn, but what we both need now is rest. Grocery ordering can wait until later—right now, I just want to cuddle with my baby.

"We're going to be home for the next little while, so why don't we get in our pyjamas and we'll put some cartoons on?"

She smiles, but her smile isn't as radiant as it usually is. I should have picked this up earlier. We've both been so cranky, it bypassed me completely.

Casey hops up on her bed when we reach her room, and I strip off her T-shirt and sigh.

This morning when I dressed her, if there were any spots at all, I didn't see them. Now, there aren't many, but it's obvious.

"I got spots," Casey says, pointing at one on her stomach.

"You do. You've got chickenpox."

"Chicken pops?"

I can't help but laugh. "Sure. It means we get to stay home until we're all better. I think Mummy has it too."

"Ohhh, poor Mummy." She pouts.

"It's okay. We'll just have to look after each other."

"And Daddy?"

"I'm sure Alex is fine. Come on, I'll pop this shirt on and then I'll go make us both a hot chocolate and we can watch TV."

An hour later, she's snoozing against me. My headache's still there, but it's eased a little, and being home with her is such a big comfort.

Alex.

That whole situation doesn't feel any better, but I've got other things to worry about now.

I miss you.

17

———

LANA

The following morning is a different story.

Casey's cries wake me. It's the weirdest feeling when I've spent the past year with her sleeping well. She wasn't the best sleeper until she was two, but being sick seems to have wrecked that for the moment.

"Ohh, don't scratch, baby." I race into the room and pull her hand from her face. Her spots have tripled overnight, and she's got a healthy dose of them down her neck and disappearing into her pyjamas.

Her bottom lip juts out.

"I'll go and get something to stop them from itching. Okay?"

"I want Daddy." Her lower lip trembles, and big fat tears roll down her face.

I close my eyes and draw in a deep breath. We've been miserable these past few days. Alex will be on the verge of leaving the country—for all I know, he could have already gone.

But we're not together anymore.

"Daddy," she wails.

I walk out of the room and into the bathroom to get a bottle of calamine and some cotton wipes. Pausing in front of the mirror, I sigh and rub my face with my palms. I slept fairly well overnight, but my tired eyes make me feel like I've barely slept at all. Gritting my teeth, I return to her bedside. I know she's upset, but I can't do this today.

Opening up her pyjama top, I tip some calamine onto the cotton and smooth it over her spots. They're everywhere. How on earth did they spread from a handful the day before to this?

She's still squawking about Alex as I cover her front and then her back. I make sure her neck and the couple of spots she has on her face are covered before I pull down her pyjama pants and wince at how many more spots she has.

"Oh, Casey. You poor thing."

"You put the medicine on the spots, Mummy?"

I nod. "Yes, sweetheart. I'll put the medicine on the spots and stop them from itching."

She rubs her eyes. "I want Daddy."

"You got me. Let's get these covered."

Swiping her spots with the calamine, I ignore her grizzles. I'm at my limit for patience as my head throbs and sweat pours off me.

"Daddy," she says for a hundredth time.

I'm so over that word. I could live to be a hundred and never want to hear it again.

"Alex is not your daddy, Casey," I snap.

My stomach churns even before she lets out a long screech.

I clutch my head in my hands. If I was well, I'd handle this better. But I'm such a mess, I can't even hold it together for my little girl.

It's not her fault. None of this is.

She pouts as I reach for her, but soon relents, her body flopping in my arms as I wrap her up tight in them. "I'm sorry, baby. I know you think of him as your father. I shouldn't have yelled."

She looks at me with those big blue eyes. "It okay, Mummy. You got chicken pops too."

Tears roll down my cheeks as I laugh, sniffing and snorting like there's no tomorrow. "I do have chicken pops. You're right."

"Does Daddy have chicken pops?"

My eyes widen, and I let her go. *Shit.* Alex would have been with us when Casey was contagious. I need to let him know he's been exposed.

I sigh. "I'm not sure, honey. I guess I'd better call him and let him know we have it."

She beams, and my heart melts.

"How about you lie back down and I'll bring you some breakfast in bed?"

"Can we watch *Paw Patrol*?"

I stroke her face. "Yes, we can watch all the *Paw Patrol* you want. I might even bring my laptop in here and you can watch it in the bedroom."

Her eyes go big. "I can?"

I nod. "All the rules can go out the window for a bit. We both just need to get better now. Stay here and I'll go get you some food."

After planting a kiss on her head, I stand and walk out of the room.

My bag lies abandoned beside the couch, and I pick it up to dig through it for my phone.

I draw in a deep breath. It isn't fair on Alex to call instead of text—the thought of us not being together still rips me in two, but he's the one having this imposed on him.

Maybe if I didn't have a fever, if I wasn't feeling so awful myself, I wouldn't do it. But I need Alex just as much as Casey does, even if it's just to hear his voice.

I dial his number and clutch my phone to my ear.

"Lana." Just my name has so much hope in it. I can't bear to hear it.

"Alex. I'm sorry for calling." Tears roll down my cheeks as I speak. I should be acting more grown up than this, but I'm sick and calling one of the few people I know will care.

"Hey. What's wrong?" His caring tone just makes me cry harder. This isn't fair.

"Are you still in the country?"

There's a pause. "I wouldn't leave without at least saying good-bye. Now, tell me what's going on."

"Casey and I both have chickenpox."

"Shit. Are you okay?"

I can't help it—all it does is make me love him more. "We will be. I just wanted to let you know you've been exposed. Casey would have been contagious the last time we saw each other." I close my eyes at the memory, my chest squeezing at the concern on his face when he heard about what had happened to Casey.

"I'll come over."

"I'm not so sure that's a good idea."

"You're right."

I bite my bottom lip to stop myself from crying again.

"I'll go to the grocery store for supplies and *then* come over. If you're both sick, you'll need a nurse, and I happen to have a gap in my schedule."

"Alex, just talk to Casey on the phone. That's enough." A tear rolls down my cheek, and I wipe it away as it stings.

"No. It's not enough. I'll be there soon." He draws in a breath. "I love you."

He disconnects the call before I can respond. There's only one response, and that's that I love him too, but being with him is so complicated.

And the last thing I can think about now.

At least his presence will put a smile on Casey's face.

I walk up the hallway and into her room. My little blonde angel, her cheeks spotty and ruddy, is fast asleep. Her mouth's hanging open, and she snuffles as she sleeps, almost as if she can't quite snore.

I lean over and peck her forehead. She's a little warm, but nothing that concerns me enough to wake her by sticking the thermometer in her ear.

I'm not sure how long this'll last, so I head back out to the living room and flop onto the couch. What I need to do right now is catch some sleep while Casey is. It's my only chance of retaining my sanity.

It doesn't take much for my eyes to grow heavy. It's been so long since I took a sick day—we had more than our fair share when Casey started day care, but the last two years haven't been too bad. I guess this is our accumulated time off.

But I can't sleep.

My eyes are weeping, not with tears, and I stick the thermometer in my ear to check my temperature for about the millionth time.

"Mummy," Casey yells.

I groan, pushing myself off the couch and onto my feet. This is the first time we've been sick together. I guess I should be grateful for that instead of cursing it, but right now, with my temperature rising and everything aching, grateful is the last thing I feel.

Tap. Tap. Tap.

The sound of someone knocking on the door fills me with hope. I know what Alex said, but I wouldn't blame him if instead of coming over, he got on a plane and flew as far away as he could.

I jerk open the door.

Alex never looked so good.

He's dressed in jeans and a T-shirt that fits him so well, I ache to touch his abs through it. His eyes are tired, but damn it, he looks wonderful.

"Hi," he says.

"Hi."

I'm sure my cheeks flush like we're just meeting for the first time—not that I'd know it because my whole face is hot.

"You need to go back to bed."

I step back to let him in. "I was lying on the couch."

"Then, the couch. I'm here now. You just need to rest."

"Casey needs me."

Alex steps inside and seems to drink in the sight of me, which must be awful right now. My hair's all puffed up from lying down, and I know my eyes are bloodshot thanks to the high temperature and not sleeping.

"I think you both need me. I'll go in and see Casey and then grab the groceries."

I'm left trailing in his wake as he heads up the hallway and into Casey's room.

Casey's hangdog expression disappears when we walk into the room. This kid was fast asleep a short time ago; now, she's all wide-eyed and smiling for the first time today—albeit a very tired smile.

"Daddy. I got chicken pops."

I clamp my lips together in amusement.

Alex sits beside her on the bed. "So I hear. I've bought some groceries, and I'm going to stay with you until you're all better."

Her mouth falls open, and where she was cranky a few seconds ago, the sun's come out as she flings her arms around his neck. Her smile lights up the whole room, and even though I feel like crap, somehow seeing this makes it worse.

There's so much love between all of us, and it was never fair to think I could ignore that.

My little girl, who never had a father, found one for herself. And along the way, I fell in love with a loving, caring man.

That's what matters.

It's as if we never broke up as Alex hugs Casey before letting go and standing. "I'm going to grab the groceries from the car and get set up. I'll bring you in a drink, and then you can go back to sleep." He glances at me. "And your mum can get some rest."

"Mummy has chicken pops too." Her lips are pursed, and her blonde brows knit in concern.

"She does, and I'll be taking care of her too. Gotta make sure my girls get better."

Clearly happy with that, Casey snuggles back under her blanket.

Alex stands and makes his way back to the door. "You go to bed. I'll bring you in a drink too. When was the last time you had anything to eat?"

My head swims and I shrug. "I'm not really sure."

"I'll sort something out and bring it in to you."

"If I wasn't sick, I'd kiss you."

His lips quirk into a smile. "I've had chickenpox. You can't give it to me."

I roll my eyes and laugh. It's the first time I think I've laughed since I broke things off with him. And despite everything, it feels good.

"I'm still not going to kiss you. But I do appreciate all of this. Thank you."

He places his hand on my arm. "You don't have to thank me. I love you guys."

"I wasn't sure ..."

"Whatever happens between us—my feelings aren't changing. I know what I want." He moves past me and I stay still for a moment, taking a deep breath.

I never had doubts about us, but I did have doubts about our situation.

Having him here feels so right.

Is this a sign we're just meant to be?

AFTER FOLLOWING him back out to the living room, I sit on the couch.

He sits in a chair opposite me. "Now, how are you feeling?"

I shrug. "I've got a headache that won't shift and I'm tired. I was supposed to make breakfast for Casey and set up my laptop for her to watch *Paw Patrol*. Instead, she fell asleep."

He gets up and circles the couch, rubbing my shoulders. "I'll take care of all of that. You just lie down. I stopped at the grocery store on the way, and I'll get you both fed."

"You're being very good to me, considering I dumped you."

Alex presses his nose in my hair. "You dumped me because you got scared. That doesn't stop me loving you. And I'm pretty sure you still feel the same way."

I close my eyes and enjoy his closeness. He's right. And I'm still scared. But I still want him, and that's not going to change anytime soon. I want *us*.

"Now lie down. Do you want to move to your room, or do you want me to go and get a pillow?"

"I can do that." I push myself off the couch, but he gently pushes me back down again.

"You're doing nothing. Put your feet up." He walks past me and toward the hallway.

"Why are you being so good to me?"

He turns and I gulp at how good he looks. God, how I've missed him, and it hasn't even been a week.

"Because I love you. And I love Casey. I want us to be a family, and I'll do what it takes to show you I'll look after you."

My eyes prick with tears.

He could have just left the country and not looked back. But he's here for me—for us.

Returning moments later, he hands me a pillow and a blanket from the bedroom, and I lie down.

"I'll make some food. You rest." Bending over, he kisses my temple before heading outside to the car.

I close my eyes and, with my headache finally receding, drift off to sleep.

All my anxiousness is gone with Alex's return. The couch is comfortable, but still not the best place to rest. Still, I sleep better than I have in days.

And when I wake, he's sitting in a nearby chair watching me.

"Hey, sleepyhead." His smile makes me feel all warm inside. *This.* This feels like normal. It feels like what our lives should be like. Together.

"How long was I asleep?"

"About four hours. Casey binged *Paw Patrol*, ate a sandwich and now she's fast asleep too. I figure you both need it, though. How are you feeling?"

I push myself up into a seated position. My head spins, but it just takes a deep breath to steady myself. "Better."

"Glad to hear it. Get into bed and I'll bring you through some lunch. I'll take the couch tonight."

I'm not about to argue. I grab my pillow and blanket and make my way up the hallway and into my room, flopping onto the cool sheets and sighing.

He's changed the sheets on my bed.

I could weep at how thoughtful he is. Today I'm not so bad, but last night I was a mess of sweat, and I could do with a change of clothing myself.

Instead, I pull the covers over me and snuggle up with my pillow. Anything more requires way too much energy.

I doze until the scent of cheese fills the room, and I open my eyes to see Alex holding a steaming bowl of food.

"What's that?"

"Mac and cheese."

My eyebrows rise. "You made mac and cheese?"

"Out of a packet. I'm not a terrible cook, but I'm not *that* good."

I push myself up, and he hands me the bowl and a fork. If I'm honest, he could serve me anything right now, and I'd probably eat it. My stomach grumbles as if to agree with me.

After scooping some food onto the fork, I take a bite and let out a moan in time with my stomach grumbling. "This is amazing. Is it seriously out of a packet?"

He laughs. "It is. It's one of those things that's always been a comfort food when I've not been well, so I thought maybe you'd appreciate it. I also called my mom on the way here and asked her for some ideas on what to make my two sick girls."

Placing my fork back in the bowl, I study him. "You told your mother about us?"

He nods. "We're pretty close. She's the wild child in our relationship, though. I was lucky to reach her because she's backpacking through Europe."

"Backpacking?"

Alex chuckles. "I can't wait for you to meet her. She's pretty unique."

At that, I swallow hard. He really is serious about us being back together. And it'd be the easiest thing in the world to sink into his arms.

Maybe we never should have been apart in the first place.

It's so hard to think when my head's still thumping.

I wolf down the food, and he takes the bowl from me.

"You're so good to me," I say.

"I love you." He stands, smoothing down the blanket. "Is there anything else you need before you go to sleep?"

I shake my head. "All I needed walked in the door a few hours ago."

His smile is faint, and he reaches out to cup my cheek, running his thumb down to my lip. "I've missed you."

"I missed you too. I'm sorry you ended up here this way, though."

"I'm not." He plants a kiss on my nose. "I've been trying to come up with excuses to come and see you."

"I'm sorry, Alex."

He shakes his head. "You should never have been treated the way you were. I've been thinking a lot about how to protect you from that."

I swallow hard. "I keep thinking about that, but I think it's part and parcel of your life now. You have fans. Some of them are going to think—"

"The only thing they need to focus on is my work. You and Casey are off-limits."

"But—"

He places a finger on my lips. "When you and Casey are well again, I want you to come to the States with me."

My heart rate accelerates, beating out of my chest. "What?"

"I've been talking to Reece. He and Josh have the same concerns about their families. We can work with them to make sure you're well protected."

Tears well, and this time it's not because my temperature is soaring. Alex loves me, and even though I already knew that, he's doing this for *me*.

Still, moving to another country is a huge choice. It means uprooting my little girl and taking her away from the only life she's ever known.

"That's a big decision to make."

He runs his tongue over his lower lip. "I know. But I'm about to take this next step in my career, and I don't want to do it without you."

"Delaney Carter called me."

His eyebrows rise. "She did?"

"She wanted to let me know I had support whatever I did. And we talked about her fears for her kids." I blow out a breath. "Sounds like there are some real weirdos out there, but I guess that's all part of the deal."

"Is that a yes?" His expression is so full of hope. He loves me; he really does. I have faith in that. And I have to have faith in us.

"I'm not going to make that decision right this second. I mean, you might not love me that much when I break out in spots."

He grimaces. "About that ..."

I raise my hand to my face. The skin's warm, but smooth. "What?"

"You've already got them, but I'm guessing you didn't notice."

I stare at him. "Where?"

"There are a couple on your shoulder, and one right between your breasts." He tilts his head. "You're not covered like Casey obviously is. Yet."

I groan. "Oh no."

"But I'll help you put lotion on them if you want." He shrugs, and I might feel rotten, but I laugh. "I think you're full of food and pills and need to sleep now, though. Am I right?"

I nod. "Thank you for being here, even after ..."

"There's nowhere else I *can* be." Leaning forward, he presses a kiss to my forehead. "Now, rest. I'll still be here when you wake up. And I'll come and get you if Casey needs you."

I snuggle down under the blankets.

Yes, Casey needs him. But I need him too.

And maybe that's all that really matters.

18

LANA

"Don't scratch."

I'm vaguely aware of my hand on my neck.

Alex.

Is that Alex's voice?

"Lana. Don't scratch. Give me a second."

I let out a sigh as cool liquid splashes my neck, and I force my eyelids open.

Alex hovers over me, the calamine bottle in one hand and a wad of cotton wool in the other.

"How long have I been asleep?"

He dabs at my skin. "It's morning. After your lunch, you slept all the way through."

"Casey." I push myself up.

"She's fine. I'd appreciate it if you got up to put some of this stuff on some parts of her, but I've kept her distracted with videos and food."

I sigh. "The way to her heart."

He chuckles. "Something like that."

"I must look like shit."

He casts his gaze over me, and I realise he's looking for any spots he's missed. "No, you're still beautiful. These spots are a little out of hand, though."

"Are they really that bad?"

I look down the front of my nightgown and sigh. They're not as prolific as Casey's were yesterday, but still more than I'd like to see.

"They'll heal. But you have to try your best not to scratch or you'll scar." He points above his left eyebrow. "That's where I had them when I was Casey's age. I scratched."

"I'm an adult. This isn't supposed to happen."

He shrugs. "It's not like you had much exposure to the outside world when you were growing up."

"I guess not." I sigh.

"Anyway, I am going to shoot back to my place and grab some clothes and things for the next few days."

I lick my lips. "You don't have to sleep on the couch, you know."

Alex sits on the bed. "I wasn't sure."

I fluff my pillows and sit up on them. "I don't know about going to the States. But I do know I made a mistake in breaking up with you. I can't just switch off the way I feel. And Casey's been miserable without you."

He chuckles. "I think that was because she's been sick."

"Maybe a bit of both."

Alex reaches over, and for a moment, I think he's going to touch my cheek.

Instead, he swipes the cotton wool down it. "Anyway, I'll leave you with this. No doubt you'll want to see Casey anyway. She's wide awake and watching cartoons in bed."

I laugh. " Of course she is."

Alex stands and kisses my forehead. "At least you're cooler today." He leans back. "Though I'm not going to kiss you properly until you brush your teeth."

"Is it that bad?" I hold my hand over my mouth.

"No. I'm just teasing." He laughs.

"Meanie."

"I'm just glad to be here with you."

I POKE my head around Casey's door. "Boo."

"Mummy," she squeals, and I smile. "Daddy made me breakfast."

"Did he? I hear you're watching cartoons."

She nods.

Once I've finished covering her spots, I make sure she's comfortable and head back to my bed. I've had enough sleep for the moment, but I'm still feeling lousy.

I close my eyes.

Out of nowhere, a shrill ring makes my heart race, and it takes a moment to realise it's my phone. Alex must have put it there at some point.

I don't recognise the number, but it's a call from the US.

"Hello?"

"Lana? It's Pania Wilson here. I'm Delaney's friend?"

Reece Evans' girlfriend. Oh my god, how is this my life?

"Hi."

"I just wanted to call and check on you. We've all been really worried here since Alex told us about that fan trying to snatch Casey. Are you okay?"

Letting out a long breath, I smile. I don't even know these people and they're acting like we're already friends. Is this what it would be like if we did go away with Alex?

No. Alex isn't even friends with them himself—they're just working on a movie together.

But maybe it's that we're all New Zealanders.

"Thanks for calling. We're okay. Casey and I have chickenpox, but everything else has been pretty quiet."

"Good. I couldn't believe it when Reece said what had happened." She pauses. "Reece also said you two broke up. I'm sorry to hear that."

I bite my bottom lip. "Well, we seem to be back together."

She laughs. "That didn't last long."

"Alex has asked us to come back to the States with him, though. I'm thinking that over."

"It's a big move."

I nestle back on my pillows. "It is."

"If it helps, you'll have my support. And Delaney's. God, she'd love having you and your daughter to fuss over."

I laugh. "Is that a good thing?"

"She's been here a few years now, so she knows how things work. And she doesn't take shit either. I don't know Alex well, but I know Delaney would always have your back right along with me."

Swallowing hard, I blink back tears. Pania doesn't even know me, but she's being more supportive than nearly anyone else in my life. This is definitely tilting the scales in Alex's favour. "I really appreciate that."

"Look. I'm not going to even try to influence what you do because it's between you and Alex. Just know that if you do come over here, we'll be by your side. Even if Alex turns out to be a ratbag."

I laugh through my tears. "I don't think he is. I'm just scared because this is my first real relationship. I don't really count the one with Casey's dad, because he turned out to be a real dick."

She smacks her lips. "Ugh I've been there. I wasn't sure about Reece at first, you know? He had such a reputation for being a bit of a man whore. And honestly, he was kinda annoying."

I clutch my chest as I laugh harder. "I did not expect to hear you say that."

She snorts. "He sorted his shit out. And he's still annoying, but I love him."

"Alex has a lot in common with my daughter. I think he recognised similarities in their upbringing. He's been so patient and sweet. It's not him I worry so much about, but the whole moving-to-a-new-country thing." I suck on my top lip. "I'm not even sure how I'll handle him on-screen, kissing other women."

Pania snorts again, but it turns into something that more resembles a giggle. "You should talk to Delaney. She adored Josh's love scene with Gabby Reynolds in that movie they made that won the awards."

"Really?"

"She knows he loves her. That man is so whipped. It sounds like Alex is the same with you, or we wouldn't be talking."

My cheeks flush. "I guess you're right."

"My only advice is to do what feels right. And know you've got us if you need us. We'll just be so pleased to add to our little group. Kiwis taking over Hollywood, one leading man at a time."

I giggle. "I like the sound of that."

"And, in the unlikely event it goes wrong, you can sue him for every penny he has."

"Who on earth are you talking to?"

I'd recognise that voice anywhere. *Reece Evans.* I might have watched more than one of his movies late at night with a bottle of wine. The man is gorgeous.

"I'm making friends with Lana, Alex's girlfriend," Pania says.

"Hi, Lana," he calls out.

My cheeks flush again. Thank goodness he can't see me.

"She says you suck." Pania's words make me laugh some more. "Anyway, Lana. I should go. I'm sure Reece is about to cook me dinner. Feel free to call me if you need to, and if you do come, let us all know when the flights are so we can meet you at the airport."

"That would be wonderful. Thanks, Pania."

I hang up the call and smile. I'm still scared—this is a big step. But I feel like I already have friends waiting at the other end, and Alex is a good man.

And he's right. We can take this journey together. Maybe he ends up a big Hollywood star being paid millions to act in movies, or maybe we settle down somewhere working office jobs and raise Casey together.

I tap out a text.

Me: *How far away are you?*

It takes a few minutes, but my phone's still in my hand when it buzzes.

Alex: *I'm on my way back now.*

I grin as I stare at the screen. For so long, I didn't know where my life was headed. I had my job and Casey and that was it. It's been so tiring being alone, and for the first time, I don't feel that way.

Alex is more than just the man I love. He's on my team, and I don't think he'd ever ask us to make this move if he wasn't committed.

I'm not really sure if I'm making this decision or if I'm so ill I'm being irrational.

But I want us to be together. All of us.

The front door slams and Alex comes running in. "What is it? What's wrong?"

"Nothing." I shrug.

He walks toward the bed. "Is everything okay?"

I cock my head. "I spoke with Pania."

He grins. "Awesome. She seemed really nice when I met her. I wish, now, I'd taken you out that night."

"We still barely knew each other then." I reach for his hand. "Besides, it was as if I already knew her just talking on the phone. She gives Reece a hard time."

Alex nods. "She sure does. He can take it."

"Anyway." I draw in a deep breath. "It's helped me make up my mind. I want to go to the States with you."

His nose twitches, and his eyes widen as if he's surprised. "You do?"

"I love you, Alex. And I know how you feel about me. Casey adores you, and maybe we didn't meet in a conventional way, but all my roads lead to you."

I squeal as he pounces, pressing his lips to mine. "I promise I'll work hard to make a good life for us. Between this job and the next one, we can look for a house—"

Cupping his face in my palms, I lean back to take in the sight of him. His eyes are so tired, but he's here, and all I see all over his face is the love he has for me.

"We have all the time in the world. And, from the sounds of it, good friends on our journey."

He pushes toward me, pecking me on the lips again. "Sounds like you two really hit it off."

"Pania and Delaney are just so easy to talk to. It's like we're old friends already."

"Then this movie deal is good in more ways than one."

"I guess so," I say.

My heart races. Four months ago, I never would have guessed I'd end up heading to another country to start a new life. But I know Casey will be happy and so will I—and that's worth risking everything for.

Alex is worth risking everything for.

19

LANA

My stomach churns.

I'm back at work after another week at home. The last of my spots are fading, and it feels like I haven't been at my desk for an eternity.

It won't be my desk much longer.

I thought about looking for another job plenty of times. But between the security of working for Gareth, who would never have the guts to get rid of me, and the endless grind of raising Casey by myself, I never bothered.

And now I'm doing the one thing I never thought I'd do.

Resigning.

I haven't told Anna yet—I like her a lot, but I need to get this over and done with first.

After waiting for a quiet moment, I walk into his office, closing the door behind me. He looks up as I take a seat opposite him.

"Is everything okay?" he asks.

"I need to give this to you."

Passing over my resignation, I watch him as he unfolds the piece of paper and reads it.

"You're ... you're leaving?" He drops the paper on his desk.

I nod. "We're moving to Los Angeles."

He sits back in his chair and blinks rapidly. "You're taking my daughter out of the country?"

Well. Knock me down with a feather. "*Your* daughter? Now all of a sudden she's your daughter?"

He leans forward. "Lana, keep your voice down." Stabbing his desk with his index finger, he continues. "And yes, *my* daughter. I should have some say in this."

Narrowing my gaze, I take a deep breath. "You gave her up. You made that choice. And now, you don't get to have a say in what we do. She's got a man in her life who wants to be a father to her. Now you have my resignation, and I've given you the required notice."

I stand, spin on my heel, and storm out of his office, slamming the door behind me. With that one question, he's pissed me off. He's never given a crap about Casey before.

Gripping the back of my chair, I squeeze until my knuckles turn white.

"Lana ..."

Anna's voice snaps me out of my thoughts, and I look up to meet Melanie's eyes. She's standing at the reception desk, her mouth hanging open.

Shit.

Did she ...?

"Is Casey Gareth's daughter?" she asks.

"I ... I ..."

Gareth's door squeaks as it opens. "Melanie? I didn't know you were coming in today."

"Clearly not." Her voice is so broken that it breaks my heart. I didn't want her to find out this way. I didn't want her to find out at all.

"We need to talk," he says.

I grab my bag and scan my desk for any personal items. But

there isn't anything in this office I've worked in for more than four years.

"I'm getting out of here," I say.

"I think that's a good idea." Gareth's voice is low and surprisingly calm given what's just happened.

"Lana?" Melanie's voice cracks.

My throat closes up and I can barely breathe. For more than three years, I kept his secret. I had to. He lied to both Melanie and me, and I couldn't bear to hurt her. And now I have because he provoked me and I bit.

Looking up, I meet her gaze again. Devastation is all over her face. She's such a smiley, happy woman, but right now, she looks like someone's sucked all the joy out of her. That's me. That's my fault.

"I'm sorry," I whisper. Shifting my gaze to Anna, I swallow hard. "I'll send you a text. I'm not sure if I'll be back."

She nods. "Okay."

And then I'm gone, walking away from my life of the past few years. The knowledge of what I just did sits in the pit of my stomach.

I could stop and pick up Casey, but I need to get home, and I breathe a sigh of relief as I pull into the driveway.

"You're back early." Alex appears in the kitchen doorway with a tea towel. God, how I love this man. His fame grows daily, but he's in *my* kitchen doing the dishes. Seeing him only reassures me that I've made the right decision.

"I did it. I handed in my notice."

His brows knit as he crosses the room. I take a seat and he sits beside me, dropping the tea towel on the arm of the couch and pulling me into his arms.

"It didn't go well?" he asks.

"Not really." I sigh. "Gareth asked what I was doing, and I told him we were moving to LA."

"How did that go down?" Alex plants a kiss on my temple.

"He asked me why I thought I could take his daughter out of the country. Then I got a little louder than I should have been." I pull away, biting my lip and meeting Alex's gaze. "Melanie was out in reception."

His eyebrows rise. "Oh."

"Yeah. I left, but she was going into his office for a chat."

For a moment, there's silence, and then Alex gives my shoulders a squeeze. "You know, it's shitty for him to be keeping that a secret from her. It's not ideal that she found out that way, but it's out in the open now."

"I just feel so bad." I lean my head against his. "She's so nice. If I'd known about her ..."

"Then you wouldn't have Casey. Or me."

"I love both of you, but that doesn't make me feel much better."

He kisses my temple. "You wouldn't have hurt her on purpose. I know you. Maybe better than you think."

My phone buzzes.

Gareth: *I've put your final pay through. You don't need to work out your notice. Take care.*

Take care?

I was hoping that he wouldn't cause me trouble, but this is weird considering his recent behaviour. I'm not sure whether to be grateful or still be wary.

"What's going on?" Alex brushes his hand down my back.

"Apparently, my final pay has gone into the bank. And I don't have to work the next two weeks."

Alex presses a kiss to my temple. "That's great."

"I still don't trust Gareth." I take my focus off my phone and shift it to him.

"Well, as soon as we can get everything in order, we can get out of here and forget he even exists." He wraps his arms around my waist. "It's all about us now, Lana. You, me, Casey."

My heart pounds.

"And before we're due to get Casey from day care, I can think of a few other things I'd like to do with you."

I slide my arms around his neck. "Like what?"

"Well, your man just unloaded the dishwasher and washed what was left in the sink, so I think I'm due some kind of reward."

And then he kisses me and I could almost forget the shit show this morning has turned into.

My man.

AFTER DINNER, Alex disappears to get ready for an evening out. He's attending the wrap party for the film, and while we could have gone with him, it's a weeknight and I hadn't planned to have no work in the morning.

When he returns from the bathroom, he nuzzles my neck while I sit on the couch, sketching more pictures of Casey.

"I won't be late. I'll just have a couple of drinks and then be home again."

Home.

Him saying the word is enough to bring a smile to my face.

He kisses me softly. "I know today was hard, but this is just the start for us. I want to make all your dreams come true."

"As long as we're all together—that's all I need."

He's not gone long when I look up at a tap on the door.

Casey's eyes grow wide. "Is that Daddy?"

I laugh. "He's got a key. And he won't be back until after you're asleep."

She pouts.

I stand and make my way to the door. "Who is it?"

"Lana. It's Melanie."

My heart's in my throat. I can't hide. She deserves an explanation for what happened today. And I'm the only one who can give her my side of the story. God knows what Gareth's told her.

I take a deep breath and tug open the door.

Every time I've seen her, Melanie's had a smile on her face. It's what made it so hard to confess to her in the first place, and what makes this whole situation hard now.

Her cheeks are flushed, and her eyes are kind as they always are, but there's a sadness about them.

"You Mummy's friend?" Casey asks.

Melanie shoots me an amused look. "I am. You must be Casey."

Casey nods. "I waiting for my daddy to come home."

"She's waiting for Alex," I rush to say. "He's gone to the wrap party for his movie, but he's not due home any time soon if you want to talk. I can make us coffee?"

She shakes her head. "I don't need a coffee, but I would like to have a quick word."

"Sure. Come in."

I step back and let her in.

I lead her to the couch and we sit. Casey tries to climb onto my lap.

"How about you go and play in your room for a minute? Mummy has to talk to Mrs Turner."

Casey grins and nods. "Okay."

She runs down the hallway and we both watch her leave.

"She's beautiful," Melanie says.

I nod. "She is. She's the very best of me."

"She's all you. That hair and those eyes." She tilts her head. "Gareth told me everything. We were going through a rough patch with him leaving his job and all the uncertainty of the future. And then he lied to you."

I suck on my bottom lip. "He did. And when I met you, I felt even worse because you were so nice—*are* so nice. I didn't want this, Melanie. Not telling you wasn't about any loyalty to Gareth; it was because I didn't want to hurt you."

She lets out a long breath. "I'm glad I know. But I wish someone had told me sooner."

"I'm so sorry. I feel awful."

Melanie shakes her head. "Don't. I'm not sure what I'm going to do, but I do know it's not your fault. Maybe you could have told me, but Gareth could have as well. He lied to both of us." She sighs.

"What will you do now?"

Her eyes fill with tears. "I'm sorry. I ... we just started IVF and I'm a bit of a mess."

"It's okay. I think you're entitled to be upset."

She takes a moment to steady herself. "I've given him a choice. If he wants our marriage to work, he needs to let you and Casey go without trying to make it difficult."

I can't breathe. "You would do that?"

Her sad smile almost brings me to tears. "I think the most important person in all of this is Casey. And I know Gareth signed his parental rights away, but I also know he's pissed that you're taking her out of the country. But he's married to *me*, and today, he committed to making this work. And it won't work if he messes with her life."

"Thank you," I whisper.

"I hope everything goes well for you and Casey."

Watching her leave eases the knot in my stomach, but it's awkward. Gareth could still try and make my life difficult before I go, which means we need to get everything sorted and get out of here as soon as we can.

I want us both out of his reach as soon as possible.

20

ALEX

I still can't quite believe it, but we're on our way to LA.

As a family.

Melanie's visit got Lana moving fast on arranging everything. She and Casey had no passports, but it only took a few days to sort that out. They didn't have a lot to pack after we sold all the household items they didn't need.

A shipping company is taking care of the items we are sending over, and it's just us and our suitcases on a long-haul flight across the world.

"Daddy, is *Paw Patrol* on here?" Casey points at the onboard entertainment screen.

"I'm not sure, sweetheart. Let's take a look."

Within minutes, she's glued to the screen, headphones on, watching something that's apparently not *Paw Patrol*, but will work for the trip. Or until she falls asleep.

She's handled all of this like a pro. Casey had never been on a plane until yesterday, when we flew to Auckland. That trip took an hour. This one from Auckland to Los Angeles is twelve hours. I'm not sure what we'll do when she inevitably gets bored, but I'm sure we'll work it out.

As it turns out, Lana's never been on a plane either, so this is a whole new experience for her also.

I love that I'm the one who gets to share all this with them. And that it's just the start for us. My girls will have a chance to see the world if this upcoming movie does what I hope it does for my career.

Halfway through the flight, both of them are asleep, and I'm well on the way to joining them.

My life feels complete. I've got my girls and my career is going in the direction I want it to. Everything is coming together.

I rouse as the plane shudders to a halt. Casey's already wide awake and staring at me with those big blue eyes of hers.

"You wake up, Daddy?" she asks.

I reach out and stroke her cheek. "I did. The plane just landed."

Lana stretches. "I think we all had a good sleep. I'm not sure we'll be any good tonight."

"I'm always good." I hold up my palms.

She rolls her eyes. "You are *so* much trouble."

"I good too." Casey looks between us and Lana laughs softly.

"Yes, my love. You're always good."

IT FEELS like it takes forever to get off the plane, get our luggage, go through immigration, and walk out into the airport.

Lana's eyes grow wide, and it takes a second more for me to see why.

Reece and Josh stand to the side at arrivals with a piece of cardboard that says 'Alex and family' on it. My heart swells at the sight. Beside Josh is a girl—she's older than Casey by quite a bit. It must be his older daughter.

"Is that Josh Carter?" Lana asks.

"Surprise."

Her mouth falls open. "Oh my God. I knew you were working with him, but …"

"You've become friends with his wife. They offered to pick us up. I couldn't say no."

She comes to a halt, staring and gaping. But all I can do in response is smile. "You mean I get to meet Delaney today?"

"Yes, angel. We're going to their house to relax and have dinner. Then onto the hotel." I place my hand on her arm. "So let's get moving and not let them think we're weirdos."

"Oh, I think it's already too late for that." She laughs.

I look back over toward Reece and Josh. They're looking directly at us and exchanging awkward glances.

Pushing our luggage trolley, I lead my girls toward them.

Reece grins as we draw closer. "Alex. I'm guessing you didn't tell Lana we'd be here?"

I shake my head. "It was a surprise."

Turning, I'm bemused by Lana's awestruck expression. There's a part of me that's irritated she didn't look at me that way when we met, but then again, our meeting was more awkward than anything else.

"I'm Josh." Josh holds out his hand.

"It's so great to finally meet you." I grasp it. He shakes my hand firmly, and there's a warmth in his smile that gives me confidence. I'm so looking forward to working with him.

"You too," Josh says. "I guess that makes you Lana."

She nods, still wide-eyed.

Josh's daughter steps forward and looks straight at Casey.

"Hi Casey. I'm Amelia."

"Melia." Casey says.

that's going on. And you are talented—so insanely talented. I'm so sorry for how I reacted, Lana."

Blinking back the tears, I sniff. "I felt awkward about it when she suggested it, but I love this so much. I just wanted you to be as happy as I am."

He takes a step forward. "I am. And I need to talk to Josh about taking some time out so we can get our banking sorted and start looking at houses of our own."

"Really?"

Alex nods. "It won't be in this neighbourhood, but ..."

I throw my arms around his neck and hold on tight. He presses a kiss to my ear.

"I love you, Lana. I don't know how things are going to go in the future, but right now, we're in a good position and I want to make the most of it."

Leaning my head against his, I close my eyes. "It was good until your mother's announcement."

He gently dislodges my arms from around his neck. "It was. I'm stressed and not being fair on you. I'm so proud of you, and Delaney's right. You could start a business with your art, and now is the time to do it—while everything else is going good. Plus, having Delaney backing you will help, the Carter name opens a lot of doors in this town."

"I never thought of that."

Alex kisses me on the nose. "Let's go to bed and I'll talk to Josh tomorrow. We should get our finances sorted before Christmas so you can go shopping. I'm sure you're dying to."

I grin. "This is going to be the best Christmas ever."

"Our first as a family." And then he kisses me, and any concerns go flying out of my head.

At least for today.

27

LANA

Christmas isn't the family event I'd hoped for. In the back of my head, I'd pictured some big reunion between Alex and Reece, brought together by the spirit of Christmas. But as it turns out, Reece has some place he goes, and this is the first year he's shared it with Pania.

But not Alex.

Alex assures me that the movie has gone well despite this rift —once they're on set, Reece plays his scenes to perfection.

Outside of that, they have no relationship.

I'm also tired and cranky. I haven't felt so awful since I had chickenpox, and I know that's not why I'm unwell.

It's almost a relief that Reece is away. It's like a weight has been lifted on the Carter household, and with him not coming back until after New Year, Alex has a week of just not having to worry about their relationship.

Not that it'll last for long.

By the New Year, I'm still not feeling that great when I realise that in all the time I've been here, I haven't had to buy any sanitary products. I haven't bought my own groceries in all that time, so it's bypassed me, and I've had so many distractions that I can't believe I didn't notice.

But then again, I didn't have to worry about pregnancy until I met Alex after being celibate for so long.

Oops.

Shit.

Borrowing Delaney's car, I head to the nearest pharmacy to buy a pregnancy test. Alex is already back at work, so he's not home, and Delaney takes care of Casey while I tell her I'm heading out out for some "fresh air". We're close enough that I'd confide just about anything in her, but not this.

"Did you get everything you wanted?" she asks when I walk back in.

"Yeah. I miss so much from home. It's hard to find what I want, but I got there." I hold up the small bag of groceries I picked up at the same time.

She waves a hand. "Tell me about it. Nothing's the same here. Sometimes I buy online and have food shipped because I can't find the equivalent. It's what makes me homesick."

"Mummy, you back." Casey latches onto my leg. "What you buy?"

"Just some snacks. I found some new things for us to try."

Her eyes widen. I've been glad that staying here has meant that it's not been a huge adjustment food-wise for Casey. She's pretty good—except sometimes with vegetables, but Delaney's cooking has been similar to what we ate at home.

"I want to go in the car." She frowns.

"I'll tell you what—how about next time we go for a drive? Just you and me."

"And Daddy?"

I ruffle her hair. "And Daddy."

"I miss him."

I roll my eyes. "Casey Maitland. He'll be home tonight. You'll see him then."

She lets out a loud sigh, her hand on her heart before returning to the table where Delaney's laid out some books for her.

"Melly is going to follow in her father's footsteps, I think. Maybe Casey is the same?" Delaney says.

"Her father's not an actor, but he's pretty good at being dramatic."

She snorts. "I shouldn't laugh."

"Anyway, I'm going to go and have a shower and then I'll take over the child watch."

Delaney smiles. "Sounds good to me. I might pop out and do some shopping of my own before picking up Melly." She smacks her lips together. "I like having you here, Lana. I'm going to miss you when you move out."

"Me too. Your friendship has made things so much easier."

She tilts her head. "Hopefully you won't be too far away. It's been Pania and me for a long time, but I kinda like us being the three musketeers."

It's hard to breathe when she puts it like that. For the first time in my life, I feel like I've got good friends who support me.

And it's happened because I followed my heart.

I don't ever want to look back.

In the quiet of the bathroom, I pull out the test.

My thoughts take me back to that frightened eighteen-year-old, in a relationship with a much older man, who freaked out at the thought of being pregnant.

I'm no longer that person.

Over time, I've become stronger. I don't think I was ever in love with Gareth. He swept me away until I lost myself, and then I crashed hard before picking myself up.

I'm not sure how Alex will take the news if I am pregnant, but I do know how he feels about me. And this time, I have friends who love and support me. I'm not alone. No matter what happens, I'll be okay.

After I've taken the test, it takes a couple of minutes for it to show the result.

I breathe in through my nose and out through my mouth, trying to keep myself calm.

Even if my life is different now, it doesn't make this whole thing any less stressful.

Two lines.

My heart skips a beat.

I tuck the test away in my bedside drawer, keeping it until the right time comes to tell Alex. He's still under a lot of pressure making this movie and miserable about Reece. I want this news to bring joy to him, not pile more pressure on top.

And when he does come home, it's been a day full of action sequences, and he's so tired that he falls asleep as soon as his head hits the pillow.

Tomorrow will be the day.

28

ALEX

Life moves on. It has to.

As time passes, we have no reason to stay with Josh and Delaney anymore. We can't yet afford to live in their neighbourhood, but I've got a lead on a house that's not too far away.

I still worry about keeping things together. We've been here three months, and things have been screwed up enough.

My focus has to be on what's important, and that's not just my career. I made a commitment to Lana and Casey when I moved them here, and I'll be damned if I'll let them down.

Watching Lana sleeping is still one of my favourite pastimes, and today I'm not on set so, for a change, I have time to lie here and indulge.

Her nose twitches in her sleep, and I reach out and stroke that wispy blonde hair that drew me to her in the first place.

There are times when I feel like I'm failing at everything, but Lana and Casey always bring me 'round to seeing that I'm not. Things haven't quite gone the way I thought they would, but aside from the lack of camaraderie with Reece, life is good.

She stretches her neck, opens one eye and smiles. "Good morning."

"It's time you woke up. I've got a surprise for you today."

Lana leans over, and I kiss her softly. "What is it?"

"It wouldn't be a surprise if I told you what it was."

She shakes her head and rolls over to look at the bedside clock. "It's still early. Casey won't be awake yet."

"Is that a hint?"

"Maybe." Lana laughs as I drop below the covers, taking soft bites of her thighs until I get into position to go down on her.

"You know I love this so much," she murmurs, her voice thick with sleep.

"I know you do. It's my favourite way to wake you up properly."

I'm so aware I haven't been as attentive to her while I've been working. Lana's felt the strain of everything going on as much as I have.

But now I have her beneath me, arching her back and making those whimpering sounds in the back of her throat as I tongue her clit, and my world's back in balance.

"I need you inside me," she whispers.

After sliding on a condom, I spoon her, sliding my cock into her in one slick movement that leaves her gasping.

"Alex." She cries out my name, and not for the first time, I am relieved that the soundproofing in these rooms seems solid.

We move as one, joined together. I grasp her breast, teasing her nipple with my thumb until it's pebbled and ready for my tongue. She rolls slightly back to give me access, running her fingers through my hair as I suckle at her breast.

And when I come, I pull her so hard against me that she lets out a squeal and we laugh between kisses. How I love this woman.

After we both visit the bathroom, she snuggles back beside me and I hold her tight.

"What's this surprise?" she asks.

"We're going to look at a house. I called an agent last week as I saw something I liked online and wanted to follow it up."

Her eyes widen. "A house?"

"We can't stay here forever. And it'll get us more settled." I sweep my tongue across my lower lip. "There's even enough room to set up a studio there for you."

"Oh, Alex." She pulls my face towards hers and kisses me.

"And then when you cry out my name, there's no risk of our friends hearing it."

For the first time in a while, her cheeks pink up. "No. Do you think ...?"

"If they do, they don't say anything. But yeah, a bit more privacy would be nice."

She laughs against my skin. "Sounds wonderful."

"We'll take Casey to look at it too. I want both opinions."

Her smile warms me in a way I haven't felt in what seems like forever. "Making decisions as a family. I love it."

"It's the only way we're going to do things from here on in."

AFTER BREAKFAST, we take a drive to the house. It's about twenty minutes away from where we're staying, so close enough that we can visit our friends, but also in an area we can afford.

If I can land the kind of roles I want, then one day we can move closer, but for now, this works.

Lana's mouth falls open as I pull up outside the house.

It's nothing like Josh's place—it's a one-level, four-bedroom house with an office and a sleepout. But it has a lawn front and back, with plenty of room for Casey to play, and high fencing to keep people from observing us from the street.

"Is this it?" she asks.

"This is it." I grin. "Looks like the agent is here."

A tall, dark-haired man steps out of a late-model BMW in the driveway and walks toward us as we get out of the car. "Alex Stone? I'm Gregory Ross."

I shake his extended hand. "Great to meet you. This is Lana and Casey."

"Hi, ladies."

Lana smiles. Casey disappears behind Lana's leg, suddenly shy.

"Let's go take a look," Gregory says.

My head spins when we step in the front door. This is real.

I can buy this place without having a mortgage to worry about and create a real home with my girls. A lump forms in my throat, making it hard to swallow.

Lana gasps at the polished wooden floors, and then again at the walk-in wardrobe in our room.

"I'll leave you to have a closer look for yourselves." Gregory smiles, and I pause for a moment before turning toward Lana.

"Four bedrooms, and Casey can be right next to us if you want her to be. Plus, some room for future expansion. If you want to," I say.

Lana clasps one of my hands in hers. "Is that your way of telling me you want to expand our family?"

I swallow hard. "Not right now, but I know what it was like to grow up without siblings. Can you imagine Casey with a baby sister or brother?"

Lana seems to bite back tears. "When that happens, she'll be so excited."

"She will be. And one day, we'll do it. If you want."

Her smile grows. "I want."

"So, the house …? We can keep looking if it's not right."

She sighs, her brows knitting. "Don't you get it?"

Her eyes search mine, but I'm none the wiser.

"Get what?"

"We love *you*, Alex. It doesn't matter where we are as long as we're together. We're a family."

My heart thuds, and I take Lana's hands in mine and squeeze them. "What about the house?"

"I love the damn house. It's so much bigger than the one we were renting back home, and there's a proper garden for Casey to play in. This house is so us."

I swallow hard. "I'm glad you like it. I was worried you'd want to be closer to Pania and Delaney."

Her smile gives me so much hope. "Those two Skype each other from across the road. Distance doesn't matter, and it's not that far to visit. I'm sure we can keep our friendship from here."

I laugh, leaning forward and kissing her on the nose. "I just want you to be happy."

"I *am* happy. All I need is you and Casey."

I bring one of her hands to my lips and brush a kiss across her knuckles. "When I travel, I want you with me."

"And we'll be right there. There are still a couple more years until Casey starts school and then I don't know what we'll do, but right here and now, there's nothing stopping us."

"You want to know the best thing about this place?"

"What?" Her eyes shine with happiness.

"It'll be all ours."

29

LANA

We're still a couple of weeks from being able to take possession of the house.

I spend the time poring over websites to work out how I want to decorate it. We're starting this from scratch, so we need to buy everything. And for once, money's not as tight as it's always been.

That doesn't stop me from looking for bargains.

And Delaney is brilliant at helping me find those. She's been here long enough to know where to get good prices on things, and Alex and I are well below the budget we set.

Alex leaves before dawn for work. I'm still half asleep as I smile and murmur to him to have a good day. With Casey not in day care anymore, I get to sleep in. We'll get into a new routine once we're in the house, so for the moment, I'm just relaxing and making the most of not having a job to get to every morning.

I'm no longer sure why I was so nervous. Delaney, Pania, and I have settled into a friendship. Having them around seems to have eased any feelings of homesickness, and I'm looking forward—not back.

Pania works most days, but Delaney and I spend our time together with Casey and Addison while Amelia's at school. I think about home every now and then, but it already doesn't feel like home anymore. Everything Casey and I need is right here.

"Mummy."

The door flies open, and Casey runs into the room. She leaps onto the bed and snuggles down under the covers with me.

"Morning, baby."

"Mummy, Laney's making pancakes for breakfast."

"Is she?"

She nods and then buries her face in my side.

"Is that a hint for me to get up so we can have some?"

Casey giggles. She loves spending her days with me, and I feel the same way. Being a working parent is tough—you miss so much just trying to keep a roof over your head. But now, I don't need to miss a moment. It's a huge privilege I don't intend to waste.

"I'll take that as a yes. Give me a minute to cuddle with you and then we'll go get something to eat. Okay?"

"Okay," she whispers.

I wrap my arms around her and hold her tight. "I love you, Casey."

"Love you too, Mummy." She wriggles out of my grasp to hold out her fingers. "And I love Laney, and Melia, and Addison."

"That's a lot of love. I think you're missing someone though."

She holds her index finger to her chin, her blonde brows knitting as she thinks before she purses her lips. "Daddy. I forgot Daddy."

"I won't tell him."

She giggles. "Can't forget Daddy."

My heart swells as I reference Alex in that way. He's been so much more of a father to Casey than Gareth ever was, though that wasn't difficult. And Alex's so good at it. It's as if it was all just meant to be.

"I want pancakes." Casey leaps over me and out of bed.

I sit up and swivel on the bed to drop my legs to the floor. But the moment I stand, my head spins and I sit back down again. "You go ahead, Casey. I'll be there in a minute."

"You okay, Mummy?" She moves right in front of me.

"I'll be fine. I just need to get some clothes on. You're fine in your pyjamas. Okay?"

She nods.

I press a kiss to my finger and tap her on the nose with it. With a grin, she turns and runs out the room.

Steadying myself on the bed, I close my eyes for a minute or so.

I look up at the tap on the door. Delaney stands there with a tray in her hands. The scent of pancakes and tea waft toward me.

"Casey said you weren't feeling well. I thought I'd bring you some breakfast." She walks into the room and places the tray at the end of the bed.

"Oh, Delaney. You didn't have to."

She smiles. "Of course I did. You're my friend and you're off-colour. Spend the day in bed. Casey's fine with me."

I swallow hard. "I know she is. It's just ... you've already done so much for us."

She swats her hand in the air. "It's all good. I love having you and Casey here."

"We're really enjoying being here too."

Nausea rolls over me, and I place my hand on my stomach.

"So ... have you told him yet?"

I meet her gaze. Delaney doesn't miss a thing..

"I ..."

She hands me a glass of water from the tray and sits beside me.

"I'm trying to find the right time. There was a moment when we looked at the house, but the agent was there and ..."

Delaney places her hand on my arm. "He loves you, Lana."

"I know, but we haven't been together long. And I keep thinking about how things went with Gareth—Casey's father."

She tilts her head. "I don't know much about Gareth, but Alex isn't him. That man worships the ground you walk on. Besides, no matter what, you have me and Pania now."

"You've been so good to me."

Delaney's smile graces her whole face. "I've been in bad spots and survived them with help from my friends. It's my turn to take care of other people."

"Josh did say you had a way of taking people under your wing."

She laughs. "I don't mean to. I guess it's because Pania's mum once did that to me, and I hate the thought of anyone else going through bad stuff. And you've had more than your share."

"I really do appreciate all of it."

"I know you do. So, let me take care of that girl of yours. She can hang out with Addison and me today while you rest up. You look tired."

Running my hands through my hair, I nod. "I feel tired."

"It wasn't that long ago I was pregnant with Addison. I well remember that. And you just remember that I'm always here to look after Casey if you're not feeling too good. Pania's a great babysitter too."

"Thank you."

"You're welcome. I'll leave you to it. Have something to eat if you can and go back to sleep." She turns and walks toward the door.

Tears prick my eyes because I know no matter what, she's my friend now—and a better one than I ever had back home.

Any lingering doubts I had about how this would work are gone.

Except I still have to tell Alex about the baby.

I'm still not quite sure how that'll go.

THE HOUSE PURCHASE seems to have given Alex a second wind.

I have to tell him about the baby before I start showing. And at the rate I'm procrastinating, he'll find out when I'm giving birth.

He lies beside me, nuzzling my neck. His kisses start soft and grow in passion, and before we can get carried away ...

"Alex, stop. There's something I need to tell you."

He raises his head, his gaze locked with mine. "What's wrong?"

Tears well in my eyes. "Why would anything be wrong?"

"Your tone and the fact that you seem to be crying."

I let out a sob. "I have something I need to tell you and I'm scared."

He shakes his head, brushing a hand down my cheek. "There's nothing you should be scared to tell me. Just think about it, babe. We're about to move into our first home, and I've got job offers coming from all over the place. Things are happening for us."

I sniff, licking my lips and tasting the salt of my tears. "I'm pregnant."

Alex—my Alex doesn't even skip a beat. "Then it's just as well our house has four bedrooms."

I'm not sure if it's relief or something else, but I burst out laughing, and he shrugs.

"You and Casey are my whole world. And this little one will be just as loved."

I draw in a deep breath and hiccough. "I thought you might have been angry. It's not like we've been together that long."

"You've met my mother. She raised me to take things in my stride. Do you really think a baby's going to faze me?" His gaze sweeps over me. "You didn't do this alone."

I swallow hard. "I still didn't know how you'd take it."

"Well, now you do." He wipes my tears away with this thumb

and leans over to kiss me softly. "I'm not Gareth, Lana, and I'll never treat you the way he did. I love you."

"You've just had so much to cope with lately."

He nods. "And I'll deal with it. But none of it has anything to do with you and Casey. You're my family. Fuck everyone else."

At that, I laugh, and he laughs too.

And then he holds me tight and whispers words of love in my ear for me and our baby.

I always knew he was the right choice.

30

LANA

Before we move, there's one thing left to do. And apparently, I'm the only one who can do it.

Pania's exasperated by Reece not wanting to address the whole *half-brother* situation.

Alex pretends he's okay but puts up a front to hide his sadness over Reece not wanting to talk about it.

Josh and Delaney are as wonderful as always, but they're not getting anywhere.

I wait until Pania comes over to watch *Grey's Anatomy* with Delaney—their weekly tradition—and then sneak across the road to Pania and Reece's house. The kids are in bed, and Josh and Alex are deep in conversation. No one will miss me for a while.

While I know I'd have support in this, I don't really want anyone to interfere with me tearing a strip off Reece. I'm so over this and I want this settled.

I've never been a confrontational person. The only person who brought that out in me was Gareth, and it was usually because he seemed to do his best to provoke me into fighting back.

Taking a deep breath, I rap on the door.

It takes a few moments, but my heart races at the sound of footsteps.

The door swings open, and Reece is there.

"Lana? What are you doing here?" He leans out the door and looks around. "It's just you?"

"Alex isn't with me. I want to talk."

He shrugs. "Sure. Come in."

I follow him inside. For all the time I've been staying with Delaney, I've never been inside Pania and Reece's house. It's just as beautiful as Delaney and Josh's home, and it's all a little overwhelming.

"What's up?" he asks, taking a seat in an armchair in the living room and indicating I should sit on the couch.

I take a seat. "You need to sort this thing out with Alex."

Reece frowns. "I think that's between me and him."

"It would be if you would just talk to him." I narrow my gaze. "None of this is his fault. He didn't know either. And I've just about had enough of him coming home miserable because he wants some kind of relationship with you—even a decent working one."

He leans back in his seat. "We're making a movie together."

"And you won't talk to him outside of your scenes." I sigh. "He looks up to you, Reece. Always has. This movie isn't just his big break. It's been the opportunity to work with two of the best in the industry, and his mother's announcement just screwed everything up."

Reece's lips curl into a lopsided smile. It's so Alex-like that for a moment, I'm left speechless. The casual observer might not notice anything beyond a vague resemblance, but I know the truth. "He said that?"

"He's probably said that to you. Maybe you should listen." I bite my lip, unsure if I've overstepped, but Reece chuckles.

"I like you. I'd say I'd forgotten how upfront Kiwis can be, but Pania never holds back. Alex is a lucky guy."

That wasn't what I expected to hear. "Well, I think so, but I'm biased."

That just makes him laugh harder. "Look, Lana. I don't mean to be hard on Alex. He's a good guy. I just don't know how to process this news. I spent my whole life thinking I was alone. And then, boom."

Knitting my fingers together, I lean back. "Yeah, well. You also get me and Casey with that." I lick my lips. "Oh, and we've got a baby on the way, which is making me really hormonal and pissed off."

Reece's mouth falls open. "No way. Congratulations." That smile's back again. "I guess that makes me Uncle Reece?"

"I'd appreciate it if you could keep it to yourself. Only Alex knows so far. And you. But get your shit together and sort things out with Alex." I stand. "It's hard to have a relationship with someone who's acting like a dick."

He rises to his feet. "Just give me a little time to work this out. Things have been busy lately, and I've had Pania in one ear, Josh in the other. And now I have Alex's little firecracker going at me."

I try and stop myself from smiling, but I can't. "He's a good man, Reece. And he doesn't deserve the extra stress this is causing him."

He nods. "That's fair."

"At least think about it, because I want this sorted out as soon as possible."

Holding up his hands, he smiles. "Okay. Okay. Has anyone ever told you how bossy you are?"

"Not recently. We move in a couple of days too. In case you don't know."

His brows knit. "Move? Where?"

"Not far. We bought a house. So we won't just be across the road for long."

He nods. "Delaney and Pania will miss you."

"I'll miss them. They've been good friends to me." I let out a sigh. "Their friendship has been unexpected, but very welcome."

"Well, now you're family. I guess there's no getting rid of you."

I raise an eyebrow at him.

"I'm kidding, Lana. Leave it with me. I have some things I need to sort out, but I promise this'll be at the top of my list of things to take care of."

"It'd better be."

By the time moving day comes, we're more than ready. Not everything I wanted has arrived, but we have beds and a lounge suite and a TV. The kitchen's all good to go, and the furniture that's yet to come isn't far away.

Alex even bought a new car for the occasion. We still have to get one for me, but I want to pick my own out, and my priority is getting us moved into the house. Everything is finally coming together.

"I'll miss you," Delaney says. She hugs me before I get into the car.

"I'll miss you, too, but I won't be far away."

"Things won't be the same," she says. "Call me anytime you need a babysitter. If I can't, then Pania probably can."

"Thank you."

With a final wave, we leave to start our new life in our own home. It's bittersweet, but it's the next stage of our journey. And the only way is up.

31

LANA

Reece didn't tell me that night that he'd finished his scenes for the movie.

Without seeing him at work every day, Alex is still left with that emptiness that has sucked out a part of his soul.

I hate seeing him like this.

He is much happier now we're in our own space. It's like a weight has been lifted off him now he's stopped feeling obligated to Josh and Delaney, even though they made it clear that we weren't intruding on their personal space.

Even the job offers aren't cheering Alex up.

It's been a week since I confronted Reece.

"What are you doing for dinner tonight?" Delaney asks.

I look over toward the kitchen table where Alex and Casey are playing Snap. At least, Alex is trying to. Casey's making up her own rules and matching cards that don't match. I'm not sure how he has the patience, but he just laughs and keeps trying to play to the rules. It warms my heart to watch them. He's right. He's her father now.

"I was thinking of making mac and cheese. Alex likes your recipe just as much as Casey does."

"Come over for dinner."

Alex raises an eyebrow at me, and I turn my back on him to focus on Delaney. Any minute, he'll give me that intense look that makes my stomach do flips. It did from the start, and I think it always will.

"I'll talk to Alex and let you know. Don't you and Pania have *Grey's Anatomy* tonight?"

She laughs. "We do, but Pania's skyping in from across the road, and I want someone to share my big bag of popcorn."

"Sounds great. Get back to you in a few."

I hang up the call and turn toward the table. "Delaney invited us over for dinner tonight."

"Do you want to go?" Alex asks.

"Yes. I've barely seen her all week with all this moving stuff going on."

"Then, we'll go." He rises from the table and walks toward me.

My phone buzzes.

Delaney: Melly asked if Casey wants to stay the night. It's okay with me if you want to pack a bag for her. Xxx

"Are you okay?" Alex asks.

I look up. "Yes. Delaney asked if Casey wanted a sleepover with Amelia."

His devilish smile makes me twitch. "And you said ...?"

"I haven't replied yet. Do you think I should say it's okay?"

He slips his arms around my waist. "If you don't, I'll do it for you."

Alex's hot breath makes my head swim as he nuzzles my neck.

"I'm going to say yes anyway. Casey would be so upset if I didn't let her stay with her bestie."

He chuckles. "Those two are close."

"They are."

He nibbles my earlobe. "And with her gone for the night, I can play with you."

"You're incorrigible." I laugh.

He pulls away, and gazes at me with so much affection, it takes my breath away. "Only with you."

"Casey, do you want to spend the night at Amelia's place?" I call out.

She leaps off her chair and claps. "Can I?"

"Yes. I'll just let Delaney know it's okay, and we'll go and pack a bag."

She's off running to her room before I even finish my sentence.

"I never thought I'd see the day that she'd be that keen to leave home for the night. Not for a few years anyway."

Alex laughs. "I'm not complaining."

"Neither am I."

AFTER DINNER, the children go to bed. I doubt they'll sleep straight away, but Amelia is pretty good at reading to Casey, and that's still the quickest way to knock her out.

Delaney stands in the doorway, a big bowl of popcorn in her hands. "Do you hear that?"

"What?" I glance between Josh and Alex, but both of them have puzzled expressions.

"The sound of no children."

I laugh. "Oh, is that what that is? I wasn't sure. I don't hear it often."

"Me either." She walks to the couch and places the bowl on the table. "I love my kids, but boy, do I love it when they're asleep at the same time."

"Casey was the worst sleeper as a baby."

Delaney sits beside me. "Both of mine have been pretty good.

Addison's been teething again this week, though, so she'll wake up at some point. But in the meantime ..."

"We're here." Pania's voice comes from the door. "Shove over." Pania walks to the couch and stands between Delaney and I, and we both move to either end of the couch to make room for her.

"I thought you were staying home tonight?" Delaney asks.

Pania pushes her long hair back over her shoulders and holds up her palms. "I was. But then Reece told me who's guest starring on *Grey's Anatomy* and I had to come and watch it with you."

"Who?" I ask.

I've never seen her smile so broadly. "Reece."

"What?" Josh laughs.

"He's a sneaky one. He shot his scenes in two days while telling me he was on set with you. Apparently they were days he had off," she says.

Josh's eyebrows rise. "He didn't tell me about it either."

"If I told you, I'd never have gotten away with it. You would have been pissed I thought of it first." Reece's voice comes from behind us, and while Alex is only in my peripheral vision, I don't miss his shoulders stiffen. This is the first time they've been together in a social setting since the craziness his mother dumped on them.

Josh laughs. "You're right. Anyway, let's watch this. What sort of character are you playing?"

"A really annoying one, probably," Pania says.

"Oh ha, ha." Reece walks around the couch and sits on the arm of Josh's chair. "You'll have to wait and see."

He looks across at Alex and lifts his chin. I swallow hard and turn to see Alex responding in kind. It's progress.

"I already made the popcorn. Your timing is great." Delaney scoops out a handful and drops a piece in her mouth.

"Shhh it's starting." Pania waves her arms.

Reece is incredible. It's not a huge role, but he plays a minor character featured in one of the medical storylines. I'm sure that is how he kept it quiet. But his character flirting with the doctors has us all laughing.

He's sitting on the arm of Josh's chair, a proud smile on his face. He knows how much Pania loves this show, and he's done this for her. It's the sweetest thing I think I've ever seen.

He meets my gaze, and I chinlift in an attempt to tell him he did good.

"I can't believe you did this," Josh says in an ad break.

Reece chuckles. "It took a while to set up. But I wanted to do it for my girls."

Josh rolls his eyes and leans back in his seat. "You're such a suck-up."

"Yeah, but this is worth mega brownie points." Delaney drops another piece of popcorn into her mouth.

"I guess I'll have to come up with something even bigger." Josh winks at her, and she coughs, waving her hands in the air. Tears fill her eyes, and Pania pats her on the back to help as she struggles to swallow the popcorn.

Delaney sniffs, giving her a nod in thanks. "Much, much bigger." She croaks.

"You two are disgusting." Pania shakes her head.

"You're just as bad." Delaney swats at Pania. "Now, be quiet. The ads are about to finish."

By the end of it, the three of us are laughing while Josh goes to get more drinks for everyone.

"I did not think he'd do that," Pania says.

"He loves us." Delaney rests her head on Pania's shoulder.

"He does." Pania leans back against Delaney.

Josh passes out beers, and when a cry comes from the baby monitor, he gets up to check on Addison.

Delaney nudges my arm. "Look at that," she whispers, nodding toward a corner of the room.

I turn my head. Alex and Reece are deep in conversation, and my heart swells with hope. "That has to be a good sign."

She nods. "It does. Reece is just being stupid. Maybe he's gotten over himself."

"You did it." Pania rubs my arm. "I've tried not to push him too hard, but it was your visit that really got him thinking. He was so wound up about the past that he didn't think about the present or the future."

"Thank you," I whisper.

She loops her arm around my neck and pulls me closer. "That's what family's for."

I blink back tears. She's right. And we are all family now.

32

ALEX

"**G**ot a minute?"

I look up in surprise at Reece's voice. He hasn't spoken to me in a casual environment since Mom's revelation. "Of course."

I stand and follow him into the corner of the room—away from the others. My stomach flips with nerves. It's still so hard to think of him as my older brother.

"So, uhh. I just wanted to talk to you. Pania's been giving me a pretty hard time about how I've treated you." He draws in a deep breath. "And she's right. I've been a real asshole about it."

It's hard not to nod, so I just drop my gaze.

"I'm sorry for the way I've been acting. It was just such a shock." He closes his eyes and blows out a breath. "I can't remember my parents well. But I remember them loving me and loving each other. To know what they did …"

I grasp his arm. "Sounds like it was a pretty wild night. Plus, they were taking drugs. It's probably a miracle my mother remembered who my father was."

He snorts. "You're not wrong." Raising his other hand, he runs his fingers through his hair. "I only really learned what it was like to have family when I met Josh, and then Delaney and Amelia ..." He drops eye contact and his smile is so wistful. I'm pretty sure I know who he's thinking about. "Pania really sealed the deal for me. Her family became mine and I know what it's like now. I'm glad that, if I had to find a secret brother, it was you."

His gaze hits mine. He has such familiar eyes, I wonder how I didn't see it in the first place. We might have different mothers, but Reece and I *are* brothers.

"Secret brother, huh? Could make for a good movie," I say.

He chuckles. "I'm game if you are."

"Thanks, Reece. I hated things being the way they were between us."

"You're welcome." He gives me a short, sharp nod. "Should we go and put the girls out of their misery? You just know they're on the other side of the room gossiping about us."

I laugh. "Nope. Let them suffer a bit longer."

Reece grins, and for a moment, it's like looking in a mirror. "Oh, I think we'll be great as brothers."

"Me too."

He nudges my arm. "You know what else? That is one special lady you have there."

I fix my gaze on Lana. "I know."

"Did she tell you she came over to tell me off?"

I feel like I'm catching flies as my mouth falls open. "She did what?"

He nods. "Yeah, last week. You were all busy, so she came over to the house and ripped into me. It was just what I needed, on top of Pania giving me shit. I'd just been so distracted, worrying about what my parents had done, and didn't really give proper thought to the wider implications. I'm really sorry."

"You already said that, and I've already accepted your apology. Let's go tell the girls." I grin.

Reece turns and laughs.

All three of them are watching us.

"I think they already know."

LANA WENT into bat for me. Just when I thought I couldn't love her any more ...

I've not exactly been attuned to her needs lately. We moved all the way here and I buried myself in work in an attempt to move my career forward and provide for her. But everything got a bit crazy, and I know now what I need to do.

Across the room, she's deep in conversation with Pania and Delaney. God, how beautiful she is. She flicks a lock of blonde hair behind her ear, and the three of them burst into laughter. The joy on her face warms my heart.

The one thing I managed to get right was surrounding her with these people. They've taken her into their hearts and made this feel like home. Hell, it is home. And now we're starting our own family.

I had plans for tonight that got curtailed by our visit here—not that I have any regrets. Now things are resolved between Reece and me, I hope we can look forward to more gatherings like this. We're not all just co-workers; we're friends.

I wait until there's a pause in conversation and make my way over to Lana. Her eyes light up, and she grabs my hand when I reach her side.

"I'm so glad we came this evening," she says.

"Me too." I pause. There's no reason why I can't go ahead with what I had planned for what I thought would be a quiet night at home. We just need a little privacy. "Come with me."

I lead her out the patio doors to the small courtyard outside. Everyone else is busy, and it's just us out here. This is something

I've been planning to do for a little while, but now seems the right time. Especially after what Reece told me.

Lana fought for me.

She deserves the world.

"I know things have been screwed up for a while, and between work and this thing with Reece, I've been pretty stressed."

Lana, my sweet Lana, caresses my cheek with her palm. "I understand."

"No. You deserve better. I brought you over here and basically left you to fend for yourself while I was working. I know you had Delaney and Pania, but you should have had me."

She tilts her head. "It's not like we haven't had time together. We did manage to make a baby."

I nod. "And that's what makes how I've been acting even worse. You told me, and I know I barely reacted, but—"

"You told me you took it in your stride like everything else."

"I also had a lot of other things on my mind at the time. You should come first, no matter what."

"Alex."

I drop to one knee.

She gasps.

And she's not the only one.

I thought we had privacy here, and no one else could see us. But apparently, I was wrong. And Josh, Delaney, Reece, and Pania might not have heard my words, but they all saw my action, which usually only means one thing.

Shit.

"And now I've screwed up this proposal because I thought it was private," I say. Lana slams her hand over her mouth and giggles. After digging the ring box out of my pocket, I hold it up. "Lana, will you marry me?"

Tears fill her eyes, and she drops her hands. "Yes. I'm not just saying that because everyone's watching, but yes."

I take the ring out of the box and slide it on her finger. Behind us, Reece starts clapping. The others soon join in, and I straighten up and pull Lana into my arms.

"You weren't supposed to see that," I call out.

"It's too late now." Reece gives me the thumbs up, and I look back at Lana. Her eyes shine with happiness.

"I love you," I murmur.

"I know," she replies.

33

LANA

If anyone had asked me—even a few months ago—if I'd planned on getting married any time soon, I would have looked at them like they had two heads.

Now, here I am, getting ready to marry Alex in Delaney and Josh's backyard with Casey by my side as my flower girl.

We'll walk down the aisle together.

There's no big congregation, no big fuss.

I'm in Delaney's room in front of her full-length mirror. And what I see warms my heart.

Pania designed a gown for me. I didn't want anything too fussy, and she's nailed it. It's made from pale blue satin and has a sweetheart neckline. It's cinched above the waist and then flows into a long skirt. It's breathtaking, and I can't wait for Alex to see me in it. My baby bump, which is now clearly visible, hides behind the skirt.

The best part? Pania also made me matching lingerie. I'm wearing a corset in the same colour fabric, which is covered in the most delicate lace, with white thigh-high stockings underneath.

"I feel like a princess." I twirl.

"You look like one," Pania says. "That dress really does bring out the blue of your eyes."

I smooth down the skirt. "Thank you so much. You've done an amazing job."

She grips my arm, a smile on her face. "You're welcome, my friend. No, not friend. We're sisters now."

Delaney walks into the room and lets out a low whistle. "Look at you." She sits on the end of the bed. "I've got some presents."

"For me?"

She grins. "Pania and I have put these together. We'll start with something old."

Pania waves her index finger in the air. "Remember when I was making your dress, and I put pockets in it? And you were all 'I love pockets in dresses, but a wedding dress?'"

I nod.

"This something old isn't really *that* old, but we talked to Alex and Casey and found the perfect thing. Plus, it can go in your pocket."

I look between them. "What is it?"

Delaney picks up a box from beside her bed and opens it. She hands me a folded piece of fabric. "It's a handkerchief, but look what's printed on it."

I unfold the fabric and slam one palm over my mouth. "Oh my god."

"We couldn't take the original magazine clipping. That was too fragile. But we tracked down the magazine it was in and we had the article scanned and the printed onto the fabric," Delaney says.

"This is amazing." I hold the handkerchief to my chest. "I love it."

"We figured it's what helped bring you and Alex together. And it means a lot to Casey. Plus, being fabric, it won't deteriorate like the paper has. Even if Casey gives it some love," Pania says. She picks up her handbag. "I've got your something new." She reaches into her handbag and pulls out two small blue pieces of fabric. "Garters to hold your stockings up that match everything else."

I stare. "I don't ... I don't know what to say."

"Let me help you with them because we both know getting them on will be a struggle while you're *hapu*." She laughs.

I nod. "The stockings were tough enough with this bump in the way."

I raise one foot and then the other as she slips them on and pulls them up to just above my knee.

"Perfect." She sits back and smiles.

"Here's the something borrowed." Delaney holds out a jewellery box. "These are the diamonds Josh gave me when we were married. I keep them tucked away for special occasions, but I'd be honoured to lend them to you for today."

She opens the box, and I gasp. Inside is the most beautiful tear-drop diamond necklace and a matching pair of earrings. "I can't wear these."

Delaney smiles. "Of course you can. I've only ever lent them out once before, and that was for Pania's intro into LA society. That's how special they are to me. And you are that special, too, my friend."

I blink back tears.

"Don't ruin your makeup," Pania says. "The something blue is your gown. I know we talked about payment in a vague way, but it's my gift to you."

I brush the skirt. "No. I can't accept this."

"Well, I'm not going to accept payment." Pania crosses her arms and laughs.

"I love you both so much." A tear rolls down my cheek and Pania grabs a tissue and dabs at my face.

"We love you. Now, let's get these jewels on, and then you'll be ready to go." Delaney fishes the necklace out of the box.

"I'll go and get Casey," Pania says.

I tuck the handkerchief into my pocket as Delaney takes the necklace out of the box.

Today couldn't get any better.

Casey and I hold hands as we make our way out the back door and into the bright sunshine. We don't have far to walk—just around the side of the pool fence and toward the floral arch where we'll exchange our vows.

Alex stands there, Reece by his side. He blinks back tears, and Reece grips his shoulder. It's a moment that makes my heart flutter. They're not just biologically related—they're true brothers.

It's so crazy to think that if we hadn't met, Alex might never have found out the truth about his parentage. They would have made the movie together, pretending to be brothers, but never known they really were.

My gaze is fixed on Alex's as we walk toward him. Josh, Delaney, Pania, and Alex's mother, Ruth, all gather around as we reach the arch.

"You look incredible," he says.

I reach up and straighten his bow tie. "You look pretty alright yourself."

He grins.

I've never been so happy.

After we've had a meal together, cake, and endless photos, Alex and I head home.

Casey's having a sleepover with Amelia for the night, and tomorrow, our little family will fly to Hawaii to spend a couple of weeks honeymooning at Reece's house there. It's still all so surreal.

I slide the key into the front door, but Alex is right behind me, scooping me into his arms. Laughing, I lean over, turn the handle, and push open the door.

"Home, sweet home," I say.

He carries me all the way into the bedroom and places me gently on the bed. "How hard is it to get this dress off?"

I laugh. "Not hard, but the zip is at the back, and now I'm lying on it."

"I didn't think this out well, did I?"

I push myself up, turn, and stand by the end of the bed. He moves behind me, trailing his fingers down my back. His hot breath brushes against my neck.

"Do you know how beautiful you are?" he asks.

"I'll never get sick of hearing it from you."

He nuzzles my collarbone. "You take my breath away every time, Mrs Stone." Lowering the zip, he places gentle kisses on the nape of my neck.

"Mrs Stone. That'll take some getting used to," I say, and sigh with pleasure at his ministrations.

"You've got plenty of time to get used to it. Just the rest of your life." He chuckles, pushing the gown off my shoulders and letting the fabric pool on the floor. "Holy shit."

I laugh as he turns me around.

"You were hiding all that under your gown?" he asks. "If I'd known, I would have had you home hours ago."

"Isn't it pretty? Pania's a genius."

"I'd agree with that." His eyes run the length of my body, and my heart lurches. This is my husband. What a weird idea to get used to.

I love it.

Turning around, I point at the zip. "She also made this really easy to get out of. Unzip me?"

I'm out of the corset in an instant. Alex grips the sides of my panties and gently pulls them down my legs before picking me up and placing me back on the bed. "That's much better," he says.

"Come here, husband."

"Oh, I intend to."

I chuckle.

He strips off, and I take in the glorious sight of naked Alex, his broad chest, those abs, and his already hard cock. I love that I'm the one who does that to him.

"I'm glad you left the stockings on. They're so fucking hot." He crawls up the bed and between my legs. One by one, he peels the garters off and drops them on the floor beside the bed.

I catch my breath as he runs a heated gaze down my body.

"I only ever want you, Lana. Now and always."

"Oh, Alex."

He runs a finger over the top of one stocking. "I want to make so much money that you can wear these every day."

I laugh.

"And I want to do this at every opportunity." He plunges his face into my pussy. Teasing my clit with his tongue, he reaches up and strokes my breasts. I close my eyes, letting myself float away as he licks and sucks, taking me closer and closer to my peak— which, as I've discovered during this pregnancy, isn't very far away at all.

"Alex," I cry out.

"That's it, angel. I love it when you call my name."

I buck my hips to meet him as he goes down on me again. And this time, he takes me over the edge, my whole body on fire from his attentions.

He runs his finger up and over our baby. "I think I want you on top."

I grin. "Like the first time we were together?"

His eyes are so full of love. "You remember?"

"I remember everything about us."

He takes my hand as I straddle him and lower myself onto his cock. I blow out a breath, long and slow.

"You feel so good." I let out a long breath.

"And you, Mrs Stone, feel fucking amazing."

I laugh, and he moans.

"And if you keep doing that, I'll come in about five seconds."

I jolt my hips. "What about that?"

He laughs. "Or that."

I roll my hips slowly, and he rises to meet me. We set up a slow rhythm and he gazes at me, running his hands down my arms and then over my breasts.

And when he does come, he pulls me down to kiss me.

That husband of mine.

Afterwards, I lie in his arms, his gentle caresses almost lulling me to sleep.

"I love you. I think I loved you the moment I laid eyes on you," he says.

I laugh. "I'm not sure that's true."

"I'd like to think it is."

Stroking his hair, I let out a contented sigh. "To think we wouldn't have met if it wasn't for Casey."

"She's one smart kid."

"She is."

"Takes after her mother." He kisses me softly, placing his hand on my bump. "I'm sure this baby will get the best from us both."

"Me too." I smile as he kisses my temple. "I'm so glad Casey led me to you. Even if it was embarrassing to start with."

"I want to adopt her. Then I really will be her daddy."

With those words, he has really made today perfect.

I know times won't always be as amazing as they are today. We'll have hard times ahead—every couple does.

But we'll always have this love, this deep, unwavering love, and that will get us through. And with this man of mine and his sweet, thoughtful gestures, I know I'll want for nothing.

EPILOGUE
ALEX

One year later

"Where we going, Daddy?" Casey tugs on my hand as we walk toward the plane.

"Uncle Reece's house."

She frowns. "But we don't have to catch a plane to his place."

Lana lets out a soft laugh. "He's got another house, sweetheart. That's where we're going."

Casey comes to a stop, her lower lip trembling. I exchange a worried glance with Lana.

"Casey? What's wrong?" I ask.

She sniffs. "Will Santa know where to find us?"

Lana claps her hand over her mouth and stifles a giggle.

I squat beside Casey, placing the baby seat I'm carrying on the ground, and pull her into my arms for a hug. "He knows exactly where we're going. I made sure to tell him."

Sobs rack her tiny body as she buries her face in my neck. "Are you sure?"

"Did he find you last Christmas when we were staying at Josh and Delaney's?" I ask.

She pulls back and nods, her pigtails flying. "Yes," she whispers.

"Then you have to trust he'll find you. Santa always knows where you are."

"That's kinda creepy," Lana mutters.

"Come on, munchkin. Let's not keep Uncle Reece and Auntie Pania waiting. I know they have a ton of surprises for you."

Casey's eyes widen. "They do?"

"This is Uncle Reece's first Christmas as your uncle. I happen to know he told Santa to go overboard."

I scoop her up and onto my hip, and then pick up the baby seat.

There's not much farther to walk on the tarmac, and Pania appears at the top of the stairs leading to the jet. She waves as we draw closer.

"It's Auntie Pania!" Casey squeals.

Casey makes me laugh. She adores Pania and Reece, and even though we spend a lot of time with them, she's always excited to see them.

"Told you. You can even sit with her while we fly." I drop her to the ground when we reach the base of the stairs. Our luggage is already on board; it got picked up this morning. Reece has taken care of everything.

Casey goes first, with Lana following and me bringing up the rear carrying our baby daughter, Harper, strapped into her car seat. Her birth only deepened our love for one another and brought us closer. All of us.

Reece has turned out to be pretty clucky after the birth of his niece—I think he and Pania are in negotiations of their own.

"Is everything okay?" Pania asks.

I nod. "We're fine. Casey's worried Santa won't find us."

Her eyes widen, and she raises her hand to palm her face. "Oh. I can see why you'd be concerned, Casey, but I can promise you, Santa won't have any trouble finding us. He found Reece and me last year at the same place."

Casey beams. "He did?"

Pania opens her arms, and Casey practically leaps into them. "He did, and you know, I'm all ready with presents for him too. We've got beer and cookies, and there might even be a carrot to leave our for the reindeer."

"Thank you," I mouth.

She turns and walks into the plane. Lana and I follow.

This is surreal. I know Reece is loaded, but flying off to our Christmas break in a private jet? There's a part of me that still can't quite believe that this is our life, even though it's been nearly a year.

He was kind enough to invite Mom to come with us, but she's got a new boyfriend and is holidaying in Antigua for Christmas. I miss her, but I have to admit, it's nice to spend some time with my brother.

My brother.

It still feels weird to even think about him that way. I used to look up to him and be envious of what he'd done with his career, was so excited to be acting opposite him, and the whole time ... I smile.

"This is a bit over the top, isn't it?" I say.

Reece grins, pointing at the seats. "I wanted to do something special given it's our first time away as a family. There's a car waiting for us at the other end when I usually just grab a rental. Besides, I like spoiling my niece, and look at her face."

Casey's all buckled into a leather seat, right beside Pania, with a juice box in her hand. All signs of her little meltdown on the tarmac are completely gone.

I shake my head and turn, reaching behind me for Lana's

hand. She's wide-eyed, looking around the cabin, and I can't blame her. We're a world away from the lives we both used to live. But I'm not complaining.

"The sooner we're seated, the sooner we can get out of here. It's not a long flight," Reece says.

He helps me buckle in Harper's seat and I sit beside her, with Lana buckling in next to me.

"Where are we going?" I ask. All we know is that we're not going overseas. No passports were required.

"We're not even leaving the state. But we're going someplace special to me, and I hope it'll be special to you."

"Reece wants it to be a bit of a surprise." Pania smiles and pats the seat next to her. "Plant your arse, and let's go."

"Yes, boss." Reece salutes her and sits down, bending over to kiss her before putting on his seat belt. "You got it."

For all the fuss, the flight isn't that long. Though, I am glad we didn't drive because Harper stays awake on the plane—she'd have fallen asleep if we drove the car and then we wouldn't get any sleep tonight.

And then we land on this tiny private airstrip, but there are cars waiting for us, and even though my bank balance has grown significantly this year, I'm not sure I'll ever get accustomed to the way Reece lives. But gestures like this are often to impress Pania, and she does a wonderful job of keeping him on his toes.

There's not a long drive after that, and I confess to being more than a little confused when we pull up outside an older house. It's beautiful in a rustic kind of way, surrounded by trees. I guess it's private, if nothing else.

We climb out of the car and Reece beams. "Come in. I can't wait to show you the house."

Lana and I exchange a glance before we follow Reece and Pania inside, Casey skipping along behind them.

Inside is cosy and warm. There's a roaring fire in the fireplace, and it's all decorated for Christmas.

"This house belonged to my grandmother. *Our* grandmother. After Mum and Dad died, she was the one who raised me. We never stayed long in one place. I swear, I've lived in nearly every one of the fifty states." Reece chuckles. "But this is where she died, and I made a promise to her a long time ago to come back every Christmas."

I blink back tears. It takes a lot to make me cry, but Reece sharing this with me touches my soul. This is special—this is something that only the two of us *can* share.

Reece grips my shoulder. "Merry Christmas, little brother."

"I don't know what to say."

He shakes his head. "You don't have to say anything. It's not a big place. Pania and I have one room, and I had the other one made up for you and Lana. There's plenty of room for your travel cot. Casey's in the third room."

"Thank you," Lana says.

Reece nods. "You're welcome. It's nice to have you all here for our first Christmas as a family."

"Tell me about her. Our grandmother." I draw in a deep breath. Reece isn't the only one who spent his life feeling alone. Now he can offer me a further connection to my past—one I'm so glad I have the opportunity to explore.

He smiles. "Let's get some drinks and make a start."

Casey wakes us in the morning while Harper sleeps well. She bounces on the bed and lands between Lana and me, then kisses us both on the cheek.

"Mummy, Daddy. Santa's been."

I laugh and pull her against my chest for a hug. "But we need sleep."

She giggles and shakes her head. "No, it's time to get up. Uncle Reece told me."

My eyebrows rise. "Oh, he did, did he?"

By the time we're up and dressed, Casey's practically sitting under the tree. And there are a ton of gifts underneath it—mostly for her. She tears the paper off each one and gasps every single time.

Reece sits beside me and grips my shoulder. "Merry Christmas, bro. I don't have a physical gift to give you, but I have something to tell you for Christmas."

I laugh. "What is it?"

He sucks in his bottom lip and studies me for a moment. "You're a good man, Alex. I was a complete asshole to you when we were filming, but you were so professional about everything. More so than me. And you impressed Josh too."

I place my hand on my heart. "Thanks. That means a lot."

"So, I spoke to Josh, and I want you to have a share of our production company. That will offer financial stability for you and your family—and they're my family too."

Taking a sip of coffee, I look over at Casey playing on the floor. She's one spoiled kid this Christmas, and it does my heart good to see her so happy. This past year has been the best of my life.

"What I'm trying to say is that I'm giving you ten percent of my shares in the company."

I snap back to Reece. "Sorry, what?"

"It'll give you a share of the income from the movies we make, whether you're in them or not." Reece tilts his head. "Besides, I figure it means that we can work together again, and I like that idea."

"What?" I clutch my chest. "I'm your half-brother, Reece. Doesn't that mean I should get half of what's yours?"

His eyebrows rise, but Pania walks past him, punches his bicep, and lets out a throaty laugh. "You two are definitely brothers. He's as big a smartarse as you are."

Reece rolls his eyes and shakes his head. "I'm so not doing this. If anyone wants me, I'll be hibernating for Christmas."

She ruffles his hair "You are such a big baby. I love you anyway."

I grin at the sight of them. They're so perfect for each other. I turn my focus back to Reece. "Seriously, thank you, Reece. I'm grateful and so glad to have found you. Everything else is just a bonus."

"You're welcome, little brother. Merry Christmas." And as he stands and chases Pania for a kiss, I look around the room.

Lana sits in a rocking chair, nursing Harper. Casey's playing with all her presents. I'm more content than I've ever been in my life—all because a little girl chose me as her dad from a photo in a magazine.

Life couldn't get any better.

ALSO BY WENDY SMITH

Coming Home

Doctor's Orders

Baker's Dozen

Hunter's Mark

Teacher's Pet

A Very Campbell Christmas

Fall and Rise Duet

Falling

Rising

Fall and Rise - The Complete Duet

The Aeon Series

Game On

Build a Nerd

Bar None

Hollywood Kiwis Series

Common Ground

Even Ground

Under Ground

Rocky Ground

Solid Ground

Stand alones

For the Love of Chloe

Only Ever You

The Friends Duet

Loving Rowan

Three Days

The Forever Series

Something Real

The Right One

Unexpected

Chances Series

Another Chance

Taking Chances

Lifetime Series

In a Lifetime

In an Instant

In a Heartbeat

In the End

At the Start

ABOUT THE AUTHOR

Wendy Smith is a multi-platform bestselling author, whose book In the End, written as Ariadne Wayne, was named one of Apple's best books of 2017. She lives with her two children and two cats in New Zealand where she bases her books because she loves living there. All her stories come with a quirky sense of humour, and she cries over everything.

Find me online
www.wendysmith.co.nz
wendy@wendysmith.co.nz